5/96

ML

2 WEEKS

BILLY SUNDAY

BILLY SUNDAY

A NOVEL

ROD JONES

HENRY HOLT AND COMPANY

NEW YORK

Henry Holt and Company, Inc.
Publishers since 1866
115 West 18th Street
New York, New York 10011

Henry Holt ® is a registered
trademark of Henry Holt and Company, Inc.

First published in the United States in 1996 by
Henry Holt and Company, Inc.
Published in Canada by Fitzhenry & Whiteside Ltd.,
195 Allstate Parkway, Markham, Ontario L3R 4T8.
Originally published in Australia in 1995 by Picador.

Library of Congress Cataloging-in-Publication Data
Jones, Rod.
Billy Sunday: a novel / Rod Jones.
p.   cm.
I. Title.
PR9619.3.J694B55   1996   95-46871
823—dc20   CIP

ISBN 0-8050-4272-5

Henry Holt books are available for special
promotions and premiums. For details contact:
Director, Special Markets.

First American Edition—1996

Designed by Jessica Shatan

Printed in the United States of America
All first editions are printed on acid-free paper. ∞

1   3   5   7   9   10   8   6   4   2

For Christina

Note: Chippewa is a corruption of the Native American name of the Ojibwa people. Chippewa was the name officially used by the U.S. Bureau of Ethnology in the nineteenth century. Ojibwa was retained in Canada.

And now, four centuries from the discovery of America, at the end of a hundred years of life under the Constitution, the frontier has gone, and with its going has closed the first period of American history.

—Frederick Jackson Turner,
"The Significance of the Frontier in
American History" (1893)

The phantoms of the human brain also are sublimates of men's material life-process, which can be empirically established and which is bound to material preconditions.

—Karl Marx,
The German Ideology

BILLY SUNDAY

A man was sitting on the dock of a lake in northern Wisconsin in the summer of 1892. He might have been a tramp waiting there in his split boots and dirty dungarees tied with string below the knees, had it not been for his knapsack and fly-rod case. He wore a tweed jacket, torn at the elbows. His face was brown from the sun. The man was staring out across the lake with such a gaze as might have greeted the Pilgrim Fathers, those boats from half a world away, and not just the little wood-burning steamer, *The Lady of the Lake*, plying between the logging camps and the Indian mission.

The trees were dreaming in glass on the surface of the lake. The human figure on the dock was as still as sleep. In the middle of the lake was a group of sedge islands, each

1

like an afterthought of the forest, the last few drops shaken from the dream. All was stillness. A fly buzzed. Fish began to rise and feed. The little steamer hovered out there above the water as though suspended from time, seeming never to get closer.

A couple of men lounging in the sun began to talk.

"Who's that?" one asked, pointing to the lifeless figure at the end of the dock.

"I don't know. He comes here every summer and just sits. Something happened to him, I guess."

At last, faint circles formed in the silky surface of the water. The spell was broken, the phantom trees wobbled in the glass and vanished, and the circles spread steadily wider until one after another they lapped against the pylons of the dock. The man continued to stare from the dock, looking toward the boat and the dark line of trees on the far shore, until the bronze of the setting sun shining off the water lit up his face, filled it with wonder, a look of almost unbearable expectation.

1

BILLY SUNDAY

For several hours they had been watching the boy across the street from Mose Bone's saloon. He wore a dirty suit and a collar on his shirt, a torn derby hat. And he carried an unusual-looking satchel, like a saddlebag on a long leather strap, over his shoulder. The bottom of the satchel nearly touched the ground as he walked.

When they first saw him it was as though he'd always been there, standing in the snow in front of Bone's, with his staring face, his Mongol's eyes. His bruised, puffy eyes were nearly closed, making him sleepy looking. His face was already old. He had the face of a prisoner. His face meant pain. They were later to learn he was just fourteen that winter he arrived in Black River Falls.

He stood there all morning, snow forming a white crust

on his derby hat. He seemed not at all aware of the eyes on him from the other side of Boney's window. They thought he was just another crazy passing through, just another tramp. They thought maybe he'd gone to sleep standing there and that he wouldn't move all night. In the morning he'd still be there, frozen to the steps in front of the redbrick building across the road on First, next to the bank. The sign read, DR. LONG. BY APPOINTMENT. ABSCESSES LANCED. TEETH REMOVED. The dentist was next door to the American Express office; upstairs was the Photographic Gallery. He stood there, as if trying to summon up his courage.

There were many tramps in Black River those years. They hid on the trains, the Chicago, St. Paul, Minneapolis and Omaha line, and they could be seen begging on Main Street; or beyond begging, sitting on the boardwalk, bare feet dirty and bleeding, bearded and filthy, staring in utter misery, without seeing, without hope. There was already the same pained look in this boy's eyes, the same look of defeat. His pants were stiff with grime. The seams on his boots had burst open.

When Charles Van Schaick returned to his Photographic Gallery after lunch, he found the boy waiting for him, the derby hat with dark patches where the snow had melted, that leather satchel over his shoulder. The boy was waiting at the top of the stairs, on the landing outside the door of his studio. Van Schaick said to him, "What is it, boy?"

He held up his right hand so that Van Schaick could see the quarter he held between his thumb and forefinger. His skin had a brownish tint, the color of new potatoes. The boy wanted his photograph taken.

4

The door opened on a wide, sunny room that looked like a cross between a hunting lodge and someone's homely parlor. A big casement window on the right looked down on the intersection of First and Main and let in the light of the sky. It hurt the boy's eyes, and gave to every object a foggy aura. There seemed to be too much light in the room. He looked around at the moose heads on the walls, the glass cabinet of stuffed birds and squirrels, the vase of peacock feathers. One wall was completely covered with framed photographs.

At the other end of the room was the part of the studio where the photographs were taken. On the wall behind the big wooden camera on its folding wooden legs there was a canvas screen on which a sylvan scene had been rendered in oil paints. A cedar tree stood before a lake. On the far shore of the lake was a pioneer settlement, from whose chimneys smoke hung in the air. In the foreground was an Indian princess in full ceremonial dress. There were other elements to this trompe l'oeil: a real rowboat with oars attached was beached on the studio's blue rug. At the far end of the wall was a false balustrade, with intricate fretwork and a wine-colored velvet curtain, behind which the first few stairs of a staircase ended abruptly in midair.

Next morning, shortly after nine, when Van Schaick walked from his home on Price Hill down Main Street to his studio, he found the boy waiting again on the stairs. "If you've come for the photograph, I'm afraid you're too early," he said. The look on the boy's face made him relent. "But if you'd like to wait, I can have it done within an hour." Then, as an afterthought, he added, "Come on inside and I can show you how it's done."

He had worked in a logging camp up north, the boy said, and when the camp had closed the company had given every man and boy a free railroad ticket to anywhere in the state. For a time he had traveled with a gang of tramps. He had lived alone in the forest in northern Wisconsin for a time. He did not know who his father was, he said. His mother was dead. He did not know anything about her, except that she had been something to do with the circus.

No one seemed to know what his real name was. The boy sometimes appeared at the door of a church in one or another of the little settlements on Sunday mornings, dressed in dirty clothes, dungarees and boots, his hair worn long, like an Indian. He went down on his knees to worship with the other members of the congregation, but when hymns were sung or the sermon delivered, he just sat there with his mouth open, his eyes nearly closed, as though the light was too strong. Sometimes weeks passed before he turned up again, and the parishioners wondered what had happened to "Billy Sunday."

Van Schaick saw the boy with the abused face again the next few days around the town—at the stables where he was sometimes given a day's work; loafing along Water Street; leaning over the wooden bridge across the Black River. Then for several days in a row the boy turned up at the Photographic Gallery in the afternoons to look at the pictures on the walls. When, after a few days and no Billy Sunday, he thought he had lost the boy, and he was surprised by the keenness of his disappointment. Van Schaick finally found him in the City House.

———

The City Boarding House for the Young Poor was located diagonally across Main Street from the town's only other accommodations, the Shanghai House Hotel. Although the ground floor of the Shanghai served as a drinking lounge, its upper story had attracted a certain reputation.

The City House was painted white, well blocked, and sober, administered by the Benevolent Society. The place was being cleared out and fumigated the day he arrived. He saw piles of kapok mattresses, and two men were using hand-pump vaporizers to spray them with disinfectant. There had been another outbreak of the diphtheria epidemic.

The Shanghai had been built by Jacob Spaulding in 1846 and daubed a reddish brown, the color of a barn. It sat askew on its foundations, as though it had been eased ever so slightly off center by the prevailing wind from the north, the side against which, now in winter, snow was deeply banked. In the evenings, men passing in the street looked up at the windows of the upper floor and heard the piano music and watched the shadows of the women move behind the cracked shades.

Billy Sunday had few possessions in that unusual satchel. A frayed shirt, a cherrywood pipe, a tin of Copenhagen tobacco, some loose change amounting to a dollar and a quarter, and a Bible. But there was also, hidden away safely at the bottom of the satchel, a single twenty-five-cent postcard photograph, already with creases, of its owner sitting in a boat in front of a lake, his derby hat unraveling, and on his face not his usual expression of defeat, but an almost unbearable look of hope.

———

The day Van Schaick found Billy Sunday at the City House, he took the boy to Hendricks, the Negro barber, and had his head shaved for lice, and bought him new dungarees at the Chicago Cheap Store.

Billy Sunday did not begin to work in photography immediately. At first he ran messages to the telegraph office, delivered advertisements to the stores, photographs to the homes of clients, and it was only after a few weeks that he became a kind of apprentice at the Photographic Gallery, cleaning, carrying the equipment in the sled over icy ruts in winter, in the square wagon covered with black cloth over the dusty roads in summer. He learned how to load the magazines of each of the four different cameras, how to spread the emulsion over the glass plates in the darkroom. He mixed the bottles of chemicals, dusted the framed photographs which lined the walls of the Gallery, the faces among those stuffed birds and squirrels, deer, moose and other feats of taxidermy.

Van Schaick was a man of few words. He imparted the technical details of the work patiently. When the boy made a mistake, he simply told him over again, without the slightest sign of anger or frustration. "Do it this way, boy," or "Too much gelatin, boy." Usually, the photographer and his apprentice went about their daily tasks in silence. If Van Schaick wanted Billy Sunday to do something he would point briefly, a slight movement of the hand, a crackle of his starched cuffs. Billy Sunday watched his eyes for some sign of his thoughts. His demeanor was undemonstrative and inscrutable. His mouth hardly moved under his drooping mustache.

In the daytime Billy Sunday watched the ladies of the town make their visits to the Photographic Gallery. Scarcely an hour passed without another lady arriving, taking off her coat and posing in her blouse in the easy chair by the false balustrade. When there were no clients, the photographer sat at his skylight window, looking out over the intersection of Main Street and First. It was only after a while that Billy Sunday realized the photographer was watching the windows on the opposite side of Main Street, in the upper story of the Shanghai House Hotel.

At about that time, a traveling photographer had passed through Black River Falls. His name was Ellis, as was clearly visible in big letters along the side of his covered wagon, which served as his home, sleeping quarters, kitchen and larder, as well as a field darkroom and photographic laboratory.

This Ellis had camped out at the fairgrounds for a while, and drove his buggy up Main Street in the mornings, circled the block several times so that the town's inhabitants might be aware of his presence, then parked his wagon near the corner of First, where he was open for business.

Farm families with small children in town for the Friday with a spare twenty-five cents they intended to spend one way or another were his first customers. But there were also well-dressed ladies who gave him their custom. They dressed for the occasion, for there was nothing they liked more than to be photographed in all their finery, expensive silk dresses ordered from Chicago and New York. Besides, they hoped that through the miracle of photography they might somehow look more beautiful than they did in the photographs taken by Van Schaick which, in their accustomed places on the mantelpieces, had already become somewhat homely and jaded in their expressions.

The place where Ellis had set up, on First, just on the southern side of Main, was a place where he could be observed by Charles Van Schaick standing at his skylight window. Van Schaick stood there and watched his lost business, the ladies in their pretty hats and dresses, as well as the more crudely dressed farmers who had decided to spend their twenty-five cents with Ellis, the hastily assembled family groups standing before the canvas backdrops Ellis had fixed against the side of his wagon.

Billy Sunday spent the evenings sitting in his bare room at the City House. There was a cracked pane near the top of the window that had been covered with brown paper and the draught made a sound like troubled breathing. He watched the passersby in the street below.

The photographer was not much given to night walks, but one night Billy Sunday watched him walk down from his comfortable home on Price Hill, the same route he walked down twice a day. He came to the doorway of the Shanghai House Hotel and, casting a glance up and down the street, to see if he had been observed, disappeared inside and ascended the stairs.

Van Schaick was often called upon to take memorial photographs of the departed, especially during outbreaks of infection. Billy Sunday would always remember the first time

Van Schaick took him to see a corpse. It was a little girl, two years old, one of the first casualties of the black diphtheria epidemic of that year. The family lived on a little farm near Disco. Van Schaick had once taught school out that way, before he had become a commercial photographer.

Inside, the house was darkened against the daylight. A friend of the mother showed them with their equipment through into the parlor, a bare room with sawn plank walls and floor, empty except for a plain table and a pair of fine lace curtains. The shades were opened and bright sunshine saturated the room. Only now did he see the small coffin propped against the wall, just beside the door.

His first shock was that the eyes were not completely shut. The eyelids hung open so that the whites of the eyes and bottom parts of the irises were visible. The face of the girl was soft, white, lifelike; it was only the eyes not being closed that confirmed she was held by a power greater than sleep. The blonde hairs on her head seemed to move in the new light streaming into the room. The hands, placed at the waist of the nightdress, were blue at the fingernails. The chain of the cross the child wore had left a slight bruise, like a stain at the throat.

The camera tripod was arranged before the coffin, and soon Van Schaick's work was finished. The mother's friend had withdrawn from the room, as though a little afraid of the mystery taking place in there, in the same way she might be afraid of some new and strange mechanical invention. Now she came back into the parlor and drew the shades. Again the little coffin faded into the peaceful gloom.

Outside, Billy Sunday saw a tall, bare-headed man working near the barn door. When he looked up at Billy Sunday, the mouth was stretched in the sunlight, and the eyes, lost in shadow, disappeared into his head. His daughter had died the previous day, yet here he was, continuing to shovel snow.

A day later, Billy Sunday would follow her coffin on the milk cart to the little cemetery, those who were left of her family following behind the milk cart and the horse as slow as if they'd been ploughing.

That afternoon, in the darkroom, as the ghostly image of the dead girl swam through the solution in the printing tray toward the visible world again, Billy Sunday felt the well of emotion suddenly brimming full inside him. He could not locate the source of it, precisely: those drooping eyelids? The feeling arrived with such power he could not think of anything at all for a moment. It felt like he recognized something in her face.

The spring thaw came early that year and Billy Sunday hid on the wooden bridge over the Black River and watched the men at work on the big rafts of logs that passed by. When the log rafts appeared on the river in springtime, people hid inside their houses and locked the doors until they had passed. It was said that the wild raftsmen of the Black River would fight you as soon as look at you.

Below the bridge he saw a few of the old lumberjacks who hung around the Shanghai or Bone's, men he would sometimes pass lying dead drunk on Water Street. He listened to the bubbling sound of the swollen river rushing past the pylons, and he could smell the wet timber and canvas and tar of the keelboats. By an effect of the light on the water, the current seemed to be flowing back against itself, and it seemed to Billy Sunday just then, reminded of his former life in the logging camps, that time was flowing backward, too.

Anything even slightly unusual or newsworthy was recorded by the photographer—a man standing with new orthopedic legs; posters in O'Hearn's grocery window announcing the annual visit of the Ringling Brothers Circus to town; an unusually productive squash vine; the stallion of a proud new owner; school picnics; a bountiful catch of trout. People liked to have their homes and farms photographed, to send to relatives far away, back in Germany, Norway, Sweden.

The studio portraits usually showed the same "signature" balustrade on the stairs, the same fretwork and heavy velvet curtain. Family portraits were popular—brothers, sisters, as well as individual studies. Families with five and eight children were common. Then there was the diphtheria. Flowers. Memorial wreath. Child in coffin. Two children in coffins.

But there were also snapshots of everyday life out of doors, for which the photographer was not commissioned. These were taken on the smallest of his four cameras, a wooden camera with a magazine holding the smaller, four-by-five-inch glass negatives, covered with an emulsion of gelatin and silver nitrate. They consisted of any subject which caught the photographer's personal fancy—scenes of family life; an impromptu aria on the deck of a lake steamer; hikers and fishermen, seated on hammocks, seated on logs. A steam tractor; mowing the lawn; shop windows in the town. There was a back view of an athletic man, flexing the muscles in his shoulders and back; an unknown lady draped with snakes, an act from a traveling circus. And there were also his informal snapshots taken at the Indian mission, scenes in which the photographer took an almost anthropological interest.

On the wall of Van Schaick's studio there was a portrait of a Winnebago princess, taken some fifteen years before, with his first camera. She sat, quite unself-conscious in all her finery, the loose clothes sewn in many patterns, a zigzag of white on black. On her feet the moccasins of worked leather were open at the toes to reveal her woolen socks. She wore six rings on each hand. She looked at the camera with calm beauty, her glossy black hair parted and tied back, her dark guileless eyes, like those of a deer, her large Winnebago nose, on her right cheek a hint of smallpox scarring. The line of her mouth was perfectly composed. Dozens of strings of beads hung down to her lap. She had allowed herself to be photographed as unself-consciously as watching her reflection appear in the still surface of a pond.

Charles Van Schaick often still went on excursions to "shoot the Indians." Some Indians refused to allow their photographs to be taken. They claimed that a man who had been photographed had "lost his soul."

The photographs he had been making of the Winnebago and Chippewa in the missions and settlements around the lakes over the last three years did not feature for public exhibition on the walls of his Photographic Gallery. These photographs of the Indians were kept in one of the flat brown cardboard boxes on the shelves of the storeroom at the back where he did his developing and printing. He hid away in those cardboard cases the shapes of the sick bodies, the victims of epidemic disease lying in the doorways of their squalid humpies; he hid away the drunken women selling themselves among the filth and the stench, the faces lumpy with smallpox.

The women who occupied the warren of rooms on the upper floor of the Shanghai House Hotel were distinguishable from more respectable ladies in the street only by slight differences in haberdashery and an emphasis in their bustles. The easiest way to tell the Shanghai women was that they smoked cigarettes in public, right there on the sidewalk. The *sidewalk* sex, people called them.

It was to the Shanghai House that men returning from the logging camps went to initiate their freedom and diminish the sum of their capital. A girl cost a dollar a trick. Occasionally these sprees ended in gunfire; but most of the time the Shanghai House was a peaceable establishment. There was even a kind of family feeling among the women and the regular clientele, though not enough to pinch the trade in Dr. Krohn's Gold Cure, for any of these women could prove to be an unexpectedly expensive conquest.

Whenever Billy Sunday passed the Shanghai House, a ghostly congress took place from eye to eye, for a fraction of a second, at the edge of the curtain. As he passed, the women's voices called to him, voices whose faces remained hidden.

It was not unusual for the photographer to use prostitutes as models in his "bathing photographs." Today at the Shanghai House two girls sat in the front parlor to attract customers. When Billy Sunday appeared at the door with his leather satchel on its long strap, they looked up, not so much at the prospect of a customer but to find distraction from their boredom. There he stood with his disturbed face, not the sly excited look of a man who was minutes away from forcing his flesh inside the flesh of a woman.

The nearest girl, Fat Alice, said, "My suffering heart, it's Billy Sunday thinks he's old enough now to come and see us."

He managed to get out that he had to see the new lady. Would he be able to see her privately for a few minutes?

"Only for a few minutes?" she said, and the other girl laughed.

Only a few minutes. He had something to tell her.

"You have a message for Pauline?" she asked.

A message, yes, that was right. He was here on an errand for Mr. Van Schaick. He continued to stand there stupidly and the other girl, who had a slightly malformed upper lip, her mouth caught in a permanent snarl, said in a quavering voice, "And we thought you come here for something else."

The fat girl laughed. "Or ain't that why they invented the telegraph?"

There was the sound of footsteps on the stairs and a woman appeared on the landing. She wore Paris clothes, more stylish than those available in the backwoods: a full skirt and bustle of dark silky stuff and a tight-fitting jacket with silver buttons running down the front. Her hat, slightly more squat than a man's top hat, had flowers pinned to one side. With her beautiful European clothes and her dark, amused eyes, she would not have been out of place in a respectable drawing room.

He went downstairs behind her. She stopped at the bottom of the stairs. "You have the money?" she asked.

"Money?" He sounded slow-witted.

"Why else do you think we let him do it?"

Billy Sunday gazed after her stovepipe hat and furled parasol, the shape of her bustle, as she crossed the street at the corner of First, passed the Bank of Black River Falls, then turned into the next building and ascended the stairs to the photographic studio.

Charles Van Schaick had not always been a commercial photographer in Black River Falls. Both he and his wife, Ida, who was said to be a brilliant mind, had formerly been schoolteachers. They were regarded as an unconventional couple. She accorded him perfect freedom in every aspect of his life, as was only proper for an artist. Although Van Schaick attended the Baptist church every Sunday morning, he was also a member of the Theosophical Society.

First and foremost, a photographer seeks his sustenance in the visible. In his profession, meaning resides in the world, not the hereafter. But Charles Van Schaick had always been interested in the ideas of the Theosophical Society. Billy Sunday had heard his employer assert that the camera could be used as "the instrument of God" and that the processes of transformation in photography were akin to certain forms of magic. He had even conducted some experiments in "spirit photography" at Balsam Point last summer.

The worst thing people had to say about Van Schaick was that he did not need to earn his living, and that his photography was by way of a "gentleman's interest." What this meant was that although his fee was twenty-five cents for a postcard photograph, he accepted whatever people could afford to pay him. It could also have been said that he was a little aloof. He spent most of his daylight hours in his studio and, except for his regular "field excurses" into the wilderness, evenings at home with his wife and children, including Florence, their newborn baby girl.

There was, however, people hinted, his "artistic" side. At one time his wife had allowed him to take a series of photographs of her naked, provided that she wore a cambric handkerchief spread over her face.

Later that day when Billy Sunday went into the studio room where the camera was set up, the lady from the Shanghai House was ready to be photographed. Van Schaick had walked across and taken one of her breasts right out of the dress, so that the effect was vaguely heroic, vaguely classical. When Billy Sunday looked up, he saw that the drooping mustache was wet, and there was such contentment on Van Schaick's face, as though he had just been caught drinking from that plump white breast. In the storeroom at the back there were many photographic glass plates of ladies with cambric handkerchiefs spread across their faces. Van Schaick would have been able to recognize most of the ladies of the Shanghai House Hotel with their clothes off.

Visitors to the Photographic Gallery might often have seen Billy Sunday silently emerge from the preparation room where he developed the plates, to help his employer

arrange the props or unfurl one of the painted canvas backdrops for a studio portrait. His face didn't change, though.
He had the face of an old man, already. He still wore the
same hat, unraveling at the crown. After a while, they simply stopped noticing him. In the streets of the town, someone on the stoop in front of Bone's would say, "That's Van's
boy, ain't it?"

"That's the one. The quiet one."

And that's how he stays for half a year, quiet and
invisible.

It had been Van Schaick's habit to set off each summer in
his square black photographer's wagon along the Hatfield
Road and travel to the great northern lake. Once there, he
loaded the wagon onto the little wood-burning steamer and
passed along the shore to Balsam Point, not far from an Indian mission. He was gone for several months at a time on
these excursions. At home he was not really missed. There
were money and servants; the machinery of domestic routine was well oiled.

Billy Sunday could only guess at the purpose of Van
Schaick's visits to the woods by the photographs he had
taken there. The other evidence of his activities in the forest
was his superb collection of Indian artifacts, to which an en-
tire room of the photographic studio was devoted.

Several years earlier, Van Schaick had bought one of the
"summer places" near the lake. It was nestled into a fold of
the hill, and it looked alone, locked outside the dark wall of
the forest. It was built of unpainted sawn timber planks and
had a roof of split shingles. At the front was a gabled porch

which had as its lintel an ox's yoke, into which the letters had been carved, HEARTSEASE, and the year, 1865. Ivy framed the windows and curled around the lintel of the doorway. At first glance the place might have been derelict, with the rotting grey timbers of the porch, rusted rain gutters, lichen on the steps. Summer grass ran all the way to the doorstep, as though it might have continued inside the rooms of the house.

The house was attached to forty acres which had until recently been let to a family of tenant farmers. That last winter, the family had moved on and corn had not been sown. But there was hay to be made that summer, potatoes to be dug and an apple orchard to be harvested. The cider press had been left out of the barn and stood rusting among the weeds, waiting to be used on the unsold barrels before the first frost set in.

By the time Billy Sunday had finished digging potatoes, there were sixty bushels for Van Schaick to take down to the dock at Balsam Point in the cart. Now Billy Sunday spent his days on the ladder in the apple orchard. His employer had instructed him to be sure to put aside three barrels, for the making of cider.

The photographer was often away from the house. Apart from his snapshots of the Indians in nature, he was engaged in certain photographic experiments, so-called spirit photography, in which Van Schaick sought to photograph spectral presences in the woods.

The lonely life at Heartsease, the gloomy, brooding forest, the humid days of mist and heat by the edge of the lake, all combined to oppress the boy's spirits. In the village, the inn with its ice shed for the fishermen who came to the lake also served as a general store, and with his wages Billy Sunday bought tins of Copenhagen tobacco for his pipe. He also liked to chew tobacco, and practiced spitting a line of tawny juice, like the old lumberjacks who drank on the porch at the back of the inn, overlooking the lake, in the afternoons. It was on the porch that he saw Tom Whitecloud, a Winnebago, who folks said drank opium and got delirious, and his squaw, Jenny Four-Fingers, who sat drinking with the men, not saying anything. The couple had a cabin and a horse in the woods, away from the other Indians, who were Chippewa, and they made their living cutting firewood and selling it by the cord.

Then one day, entirely by accident, when Billy Sunday was driving the cart along the logging road (Julius Schnur had arranged the purchase of a barrel of apples), he saw horses tethered and the square black hood of the photographer's wagon.

Billy Sunday pulled up. The cart could go no further for the trees. There was no logging road into these woods. The misty trees seemed to belong to another world. It was there, at the edge of the dreamlike trees of Temple Woods, Billy Sunday heard for the first time a note sung so rich and clear it seemed to soar above the tops of the pines and hang in the sunny air. The note sustained itself so long the mist took on its colors, pink and mauve, like shot silk. That pure, dangerous voice coming through the fog made him feel a kind of panic.

When Pauline L'Allemand had turned up at Balsam Point that hot week in July, she was noticed for her Chicago dresses and her haughty demeanor; for she had soon let it get around that she was a very famous opera singer indeed, a soprano with three full octaves at her command, and who had sung to royalty at Dresden and Berlin. She certainly seemed European, with her airs and graces.

But she was also noticed for her choice of accommodations: the "summer place" of the commercial photographer from Black River Falls. She had arrived on *The Lady of the Lake* one morning with her son, Edgar, a youth who wore a leg brace, and whose dress and manners were only slightly less affected than her own. They had brought with them trunks and cases bearing the stamps of two steamship lines and some of the grandest hotels in Europe. A wagon had to be sent down to the dock to move it all.

The photographer and the singer kept to themselves, seldom appearing together in public, and that only made the villagers at Balsam Point more curious. The lady had weak nerves. People suspected that they were down on their luck, but there were different stories as to what had brought about their reduced circumstances. They heard it from the crippled son, Edgar, who liked a drink, that the lady, Pauline, had put money of her own into financing an opera. There had been a season, brutally short, in Chicago; the production had reached Milwaukee before it had folded. Its company had disbanded, the bills unpaid.

Heartsease, the place was called, because of the heartsease violets bordering the path, and this sentimental nomenclature served only to make Balsam Point all the more scornful of the silent gentleman photographer, and of Pauline and Edgar, she with her beautiful dresses, he with his weakness for whiskey. But these tough northwoods folk had a general disdain for all the "summer people." The house stood empty for most of the year, unvisited except by curious local children. They knew it as "the old witch house."

There was a large living room with tessellated windows, where a piano had been installed, and now on still nights the sound of the piano could be heard a good distance away from the house, accompanying a lady singing. The music, cool and lovely in the moonlight, drifted across the lake and through the trees. It must have been the summer people from Heartsease, the "circus people," as folks called the singer and her son.

When Billy Sunday entered the screened-in porch one afternoon, he saw Edgar sitting there with his aluminum violin and beside him the singer in a sun hat and wimple. From the wimple had escaped a skein of red hair. The leaves of the grape arbor threw mottled shadows across her face, so that, for a moment, her complexion resembled the speckled coloring of a trout. He noticed that she had beautiful hands, very white and soft, compared with the brown wrinkled hands of most women he had seen.

"Her skin can't bear the least rays of the sun, else she breaks out. Redhead people can't take the sun too much," Edgar said. Edgar kept tugging to straighten his blue silk waistcoat. He stared at the wild boy a moment longer, his slightly protruding eyes kindly and mild.

The singer looked hot. Strands of wet hair stuck to her forehead. "You see?" she said to Edgar. "Of course he is an Indian." She turned her attractive dark eyes on Billy Sunday. "Don't listen to a word Edgar says. He is a little stupid. Yes, he is altogether too stupid for words!" But the way she said it sounded as though this might have been a teasing game they regularly played.

In the night Billy Sunday lay on his bed of rags in the stables of the house in the forest and heard that soaring voice again, singing in the lighted parlor of the house. Her voice was commanding, imperious, like the voice of God pouring down through a rent in the sky. He had recognized the lady from the afternoon he had fetched her to Van Schaick's studio in Black River Falls, and later, with her breast hanging loose out of her dress.

Billy Sunday had already come to know the woods well that summer. He followed the old logging roads and the river, which had been spoiled for fishing. He also followed other paths through the woods, paths barely distinguishable from the forest floor. He collected the mushrooms which grew through the mulch of pine needles, and dug worms for his hooks. For Billy Sunday, the getting of fish was something to be done quickly: he sprinkled cornmeal on the surface to get the trout to rise.

At the little inn on the edge of the lake where the fishermen stayed, Billy Sunday sat on the porch spitting tobacco juice with the men. It was there he met Jack Knotts, Captain John Wesley Knotts, who owned *The Lady of the Lake*, the old wood-burning steamer. Jack Knotts's family had come from Canada, where they owned a timber mill and a fireworks factory, but Jack had taken to the sea, ended up a drunkard, selling his navigational instruments in the markets of Montreal in order to continue a drinking bout. Billy Sunday confessed his interest in photography, and allowed the man to see his picture of the lady with the handkerchief over her face. Jack Knotts winked his one good eye. The leather eyepatch told of an incident with a Swede and a stevedore's hook. It was said that he had traded rifles to the Indians, once upon a time, when the Indians had wanted rifles. Walking back up to the inn, Billy Sunday could still hear the other man's laughter.

When he had finished his day's work, Billy Sunday went down to the lake to swim and to watch the Indian girls bathe. They bathed at a place just down from where the old lumber camp had been, and deadheads had washed up onto the bank. As he lay there, the whoops of the girls merged in his mind with the singer's beautiful voice he heard from the house at night.

Then one afternoon when there was not another soul about and he had fallen asleep on the bank of the lake, he heard that distinctive voice again. He opened his eyes. Everything around him had a fuzzy halo of light. The woods were silent, except for the drone of insects down on the water. He went to investigate.

Mr. Van Schaick and Pauline had set up the camera on its folding wooden legs in the clearing. She had disrobed, just as she had that first afternoon in the studio. Softly at first, she began to sing. That thrilling voice was like cold fingers on him, and suddenly his head was full of the sky. The notes uncoiled themselves effortlessly, soaring higher and purer all the time. His fingers were already fumbling with his clothing and now he began to touch himself. The trees were full of moaning women, moaning for him to go on, their breathing and his own all part of the voice in the lake. A hand passed over his spine, making his skin prickle.

He felt the blood come close in his face. He looked down, and saw that a thread of semen hung there. He knew then without doubt that that voice pouring out in lovely shocks of air was something dangerous. How else was he to understand her mad act, a women who would take off her clothes and sing her soul naked in front of a camera?

Those nights he had heard music coming from the house, when he had lain in the barn and heard the piano notes from the cozy parlor, it had seemed like a feeling of what home might be. But now, by the simple act of opening her mouth, this woman had made music something dangerous, something which was against nature, not part of it, an enchantment which had lured him away from the comforting earth and into the fabric of the sky.

Leaning forward, still breathing fast, his cheek hard against the trunk of the pine, he looked down at the figures in the clearing. Sometime the voice had stopped, but still he could hear its faint echo, like the rushing of wings, or the wind in the spiraling air, dangerously close and fast. He would later ascribe to the sound borne from that open mouth the magical agency that changed his life. Music for him was a new and dangerous pleasure; the color of her voice spread like a stain in the air.

He felt tenderness for this lady observed from afar, which flared up in his chest when he thought of her; but at the same time, an impulse to do some violence to her, to take that soft white throat in his hands and by pressing his thumbs to squeeze the breath out of her and bring that pure soaring voice to an end. These were entirely new feelings, not to be quickly or easily understood.

In keeping with both her professions, Pauline L'Allemand was a nocturnal creature. She often spent the day in her darkened room, lying on the sofa, draped in silk. During these times she was cut off from the world, and she found it impossible to talk to a soul. In her room, with the curtains drawn, it was like an artificial night.

Sometimes in the night, Billy Sunday looked up in his sleep and heard a steamer making its way across the lake. He knew by the sound of its engines that it was *The Lady of the Lake*, and that this would be Jack Knotts working by night, engaged in moving contraband. Billy Sunday finally closed his eyes to try to sleep, and for a long time he lay there with the rhythm of the wood-burning steamer shuddering through the forest night, a sound which, after a time, was followed by another sound, the screeching of a wild animal, or it might have been the trumpeting of a circus elephant.

In the mornings Billy Sunday could hear Pauline practice her scales. The songs, in German and Italian, seemed strangely at home in the woods. Her voice rose above the towering pines with its swoops of emotion, soaring chaos. It was something seductive and dangerous which drew him further into the trees. Her voice seemed to have the sound of the wind in it, the free promise of the wind. It drifted westward with the wind across the prairies, full of the dry smell after harvest, soaring smoothly over low hills, then plummeting and panicking, trapped in the weird canyons. Those dangerous notes of Pauline inhabited the shadows of a wild and discordant place. Her voice became the trees with their illicit smells, the shadows of the girls moving along the forest floor among the bright lichens and dark ivy.

When he was at work at the farm tasks at Heartsease, he was aware that he was waiting to hear her voice again. He would be in the middle of some task and hear it through the trees and stop dead, heaving for breath. There seemed to be something holding him back, choking him, and Billy Sunday wondered at the cause of that.

The previous owner, a beef man from Chicago, had calculated that it would be possible to gain a view of the lake and had had an observation tower built. It had been this tower that had first attracted Van Schaick to the house, with his interest in optical instruments. From this tower Billy Sunday could see where the finger of the lake pointed north and the inn with its ice shed behind the dock. He looked through Edgar's telescope, watching the afternoon light in the leaves. He watched the activity at the dock at Balsam Point when *The Lady of the Lake* called in early in the mornings twice a week. He watched men on the logging road, farmers with their rifles; as well as other men in their buckskins and bandannas who looked like showmen from Buffalo Bill's Wild West Show.

A boy learned to be careful of strangers. There were recluses who lived in the woods around there, men who had disappeared years before, and who were sometimes seen by hunters and fishermen, half starving, dressed in rags, living like animals, and often raving mad.

Billy Sunday was working in the garden one afternoon when a man appeared at the front of the house with its ox-yoke lintel. He might have been just another tramp passing by in his split boots and dirty dungarees, except for the tweed jacket, torn at the elbow, and his fly-rod case. He did not go to the door, but just stood there a minute, staring strangely, before moving on. It was only after several days that Billy Sunday learned that their "visitor" was a university man from Madison named Turner who was staying at the inn.

Late in the afternoons, Billy Sunday took the little rowing boat out on the lake. The landscape through which he floated seemed like a dream. The effect of watching the sky on the surface of the lake was as though the water were draining the light from the air above, leaving the afternoon sky less blue, more golden. And as he lost himself in the luminous surface of the lake, he heard again Pauline L'Allemand's voice soar above the trees.

Billy Sunday grew curious about this lone fisherman from Madison who tied his own flies and gave the trout a fighting chance. When his day's work was done, Billy Sunday sometimes followed him in the woods, and learned that he too liked to spy on the girls bathing in the lake, not far from the Indian mission.

In the late afternoons, the man went to store his catch in the ice shed at the back of the inn beside the smokehouse where they smoked racks of trout over maple chips. He usually wore his old mackinaw in the woods. It was bloodstreaked, unclean looking, as though many creatures had met their deaths in its folds. And the way he just sat and stared! Billy Sunday had often seen him sitting against a tree like that, staring out into the lake toward Temple Woods, as though waiting for someone to appear.

Billy Sunday saw Edgar at the inn one evening, slumped in a chair in the corner. Edgar seemed the worse for wear. There was a full glass of whiskey in front of him. He was sitting alone next to the empty fireplace, big enough to take six-foot logs in winter. Seeing Billy Sunday, he opened his mouth as if he would say something to the stable boy. Then he appeared to think better of it, and downed his glass of whiskey instead.

Edgar had got himself in trouble. One of the local girls claimed he had been bothering her. Turning the corner out the back of the inn, she had suddenly come across the crippled boy, huddled against the wall, the evening rain running off the brim of his hat. He was drunk, and his eyes stared into her, as though it was for her he had been waiting.

Billy Sunday felt sorry for Edgar. He understood the look in Edgar's eyes, the pain twisting him up inside from the burden of that brace. Edgar sat with the rain steaming from his hair and skin, an aura around him rising like smoke. It was a face that looked as though it had just woken, full of disturbing dreams.

No one knew where the fisherman from Madison had disappeared to, and no one asked. He hadn't eaten or slept at the inn for two or three days, that was all. Billy Sunday saw his campfire, a new star in the constellation of the Indian camp. It was in Temple Woods, where he had heard the sound of low chanting. Of course, it was not unknown for a white man to "go Indian."

Next afternoon Billy Sunday heard a voice on the other side of the slashing. Loggers had been using heavy horses in there, hauling trees. There were fresh deep wheel ruts from the big wagons. He listened intently. Everything was unnaturally still except for this voice rising and falling. The man seemed to be conducting a conversation with himself, quietly and doggedly going over and over it with himself, back and forth, as if trying to follow the steps of logic of something he could not understand.

Turner was lying down in the grass, nearly invisible. He had left his mackinaw somewhere. It was hot, and his undershirt had wet patches, as though some dark substance had sweated up out of his own body. His shotgun was in the grass beside him. Suddenly he sat up and accused Billy Sunday. "You were following me, weren't you?" he demanded.

"Oh no," Billy Sunday said, with an unsteady voice.

"But I happen to know you were pursuing me as far back as Temple Woods."

"I was not pursuing you," Billy Sunday said.

"Well, I do not propose to let you get away with it."

The man looked down at the motherless boy who had one pair of dungarees to his name, who had as his name only a day of the week. His voice as he spoke now was strangely disembodied, as though he was preoccupied with something else. "That name of yours, that Billy Sunday name. You got another name, right?"

"Yessir!" Billy Sunday said. He was eager to give a categorical answer and have done with him. Billy Sunday could see the tension in his lips and nostrils, in those frightened eyes of his, and for a moment he thought the man was about to strike him. Then just as suddenly his features seemed to be filled with the forest again, the place beyond the dark river, the Temple Woods of disemboweled animals and the smell of salmon rotting in the dry riverbed in the fall.

Billy Sunday knew that sudden changes in men's behavior usually brought with them the potential for violence. But the man's voice now was gentle, almost tender. "It's all right. I've seen you before. I've seen you lots of times, haven't I?"

Billy Sunday had been in Temple Woods earlier that day and he had heard Turner's voice in the trees. It was a voice full of pain and longing, like the voice of a man pleading, or praying. Billy Sunday had followed the voice up the stream to the clearing. And Billy Sunday had been watching Turner from the cover of the trees when someone else had appeared.

At first Billy Sunday had felt the presence in the trees before he could see it. Something was moving in the trees on the other side of the clearing. He thought it must have been one of the hermits from around there, who had heard Turner's pleading voice and come to see what was going on.

But then Billy Sunday had seen it was an Indian girl. He saw the black of her hair, the pearls of smallpox on her cheeks. The girl was naked, except for an unbuttoned red plaid shirt, and her skin was smeared with feces and grass.

The apparition hovered there before him. Her clay-white face came right up close and looked at him, really scrutinized him, as though there were no boys like him in the spirit world she came from. Billy Sunday stared back in fear and wonderment. His breath came quick. His heart was pounding in his chest. He felt pity for this strange, sad figure. There was grass and dirt caught up in her hair. She looked like she had been buried. Her face was painted the color of clay, like discolored ivory on the keys of a piano. Her smell was not caused by proximity to ordure, like a stable boy's. It was the reek of an unwashed living thing, a smell as simple as evil, bacterial decay, like the smell of bad teeth had gotten into the grain of her skin.

Then, all at once, her body writhed, and she was breathing harshly, as if she was in agony. Her legs were thrashing shapes on the forest floor, her skin grew darker, already melting back into the earth.

Now Turner said to him, "These woods are a beautiful thing to see, are they not?"

"Yes, sir."

"Yes, they are," Turner said, as though he had been contradicted. "Mighty beautiful. But they are more than that. What is beautiful attracts, but what is sublime *transcends*. Do you understand that, Billy Sunday? What I am trying to discover here is no less than the idea of America."

And in that moment his face was lit up, beaming, kind of noble.

———

Billy Sunday trudged back along the trail to the house with the ox yoke for a lintel. Some Indian bark-peelers stopped work to watch him pass by. Billy Sunday raised his arm in greeting, but the Indians just stood still and stared at him.

When he was nearly to the logging road, Billy Sunday saw a train moving along the Soo Line. First he saw the black smoke on the other side of the lake. He heard the thumping of the locomotive, then, when it was close, the loud clattering of the iron wheels on the tracks. He watched the cars of the circus train pass. Some of them were boxcars, others had been built like cages. On the open trucks he saw the brightly painted steam calliope and the bell wagon. As the carriages passed by, the steam whistle shrieked, a sound like a girl screaming.

2

FREDERICK JACKSON TURNER

A thousand things can send a man into the dark; but it's always the same thing that keeps bringing him back there again.

From the deck of the little wood-burning steamer, *The Lady of the Lake*, the clearings with their rows of flattened trees looked like meteor sites. The travelers passed settlements on the shore of the great lake. At one logging camp, derelict and abandoned, the prevailing winds had shifted the symmetry of the cabins askew.

When darkness had fallen, Turner sat out on the deck wrapped in his old mackinaw blanket and looked at the stars—the Plough with its seven bright points, Ursa Major, the sign of the she-bear. The campfires of the Indians on the shores of the lake twinkled like those stars, like the pattern of a night sky etched with intention. The sound of the night wind in the trees was like the lower register of an organ, the beginning of some dark hymn.

Next day *The Lady of the Lake* approached the dock at Balsam Point with a shriek upon its steam whistle. The far shore was a black shadow-line of trees. The trees stretched north into Canada, to the ice, to the hard, final line at the end of the world. The dark wall of the forest rose above the little settlement at the edge of the lake, dwarfing it.

On the dock a few of the Indians who made their living selling cordwood watched him pass. The village—eight houses, a blacksmith's shop and an inn—was built around an old sawmill. There was also, behind the mill and the inn, the white steeple of a Presbyterian church. The inn was a modest building of two stories. Downstairs was a huge fireplace that took up half the wall. It was big enough for a man to stand inside. Behind the inn was a smokehouse and an ice shed, where game and fish were kept for the sportsmen who stayed there. A few summer places were scattered around the lakeshore.

The clerk appeared at the reception desk. He had a cold, unfriendly look. "What do you want?" he asked Turner.

"What do I want?" Turner repeated the question stupidly.

"We got no more rooms."

"But look here. I have a reservation. I stay here every year. Room Five, the attic room, right under the roof. I have an arrangement with Mr. Konrad."

"Mr. Konrad don't own the inn no more."

"But what about my reservation? I must say this is all extremely inconvenient."

"Do you have some evidence that what you say is true? Do you have confirmation in writing of your reservation?"

"Confirmation in writing!" Turner could not understand the man's hostility. "No! I'm afraid you will have to take my word for it. Look, I have come from Madison. I am tired. I wish to go up to my room now. I can promise you will not see very much of me. My purpose is to spend every day here at sport, fly-fishing."

The other man's face was held hard; then, his obstinacy seemed to dissolve. "I can't afford to waste my time on these trifling matters. I can see that you're determined to stay. Go up to your damned attic room. You'll have to carry your own bags up the stairs."

Turner looked around at the single, iron bed with its canopy of dusty mosquito netting, the old wicker chair, the washstand with its hexagonal mirror, the faded drapes. The room had not changed.

He removed his hat and coat right away and went over to the washstand. There was no water in the pitcher and the bowl was covered in a film of dust. He took out his handkerchief and mopped the sweat from his face and neck. He combed his hair in front of the mirror. He then took a small pair of nail scissors from one of the side pockets of his rucksack and trimmed his mustache along the line of his upper lip, until it was pleasing to him. He might have been getting ready for a night out with the ladies rather than a month's fishing. He drew the drapes, shutting out the daylight, then sat in the wicker chair, lit a cigar and waited.

There was the sound of quiet rain outside and the rain gutters sighed. It sounded like someone crying quietly to herself. By the time the rain had stopped and sunlight leaked in around the edges of the brown drapes, the whimpering sound had ceased.

Hours later, he was still up there in his room. From the attic window he looked out over the shingle roof, slippery with rain, to the pine forest beyond. He stood in his old room and felt the sheltering night creep around him, eating up his shape, until he was hardly there, a shadow in the mirror.

Frederick Jackson Turner was thirty years old in the summer of 1892. He was a very good-looking man, with brown hair and a mustache. His smiling blue eyes were often described by acquaintances as "charming."

Turner was an outstanding member of the History Department of the University of Wisconsin. But as disciplined as he was in both research and teaching, his actual writing was distinguished mainly by his diligence in procrastination. This is by no means an unusual predicament in academic life. A lack of publication should not in itself preclude a man of ambition from a respectable career. Yet Turner could not accept that his destiny should thus be thwarted, or that his career should be a modest one.

In the summer of 1877, and again in 1879, the young Turner had accompanied his father, Andrew Jackson Turner, on trips to the north of the state, where the father was involved in a series of land speculations. His father was a dedicated fly-fisherman, but his business dealings kept him engaged for several weeks and the son was left to his own resources, exploring the virgin forest, hunting and fishing. It was after he had returned from the second of these trips, when he was seventeen, that young Fred Turner had been afflicted with a mysterious illness which had required his staying home from school for a year.

At the time the medical diagnosis was anything but clear. Over the course of the disease he was more than once accounted to be close to death. He was weakened and for months at a time he could not leave his bed. One doctor diagnosed the trouble as acute spinal meningitis. The young man suffered visions, savage dreamlike interludes, and he often screamed with the severe headaches.

He lay in his sickbed, reading *Paradise Lost* and *Don Juan*, Dickens, *The Scarlet Letter* and Longfellow's *Song of Hiawatha*. He also surrounded himself with his beloved maps, which he had spent hours poring over since his childhood. Turner's hometown, Portage, was the site where Marquette and Jolliet had carried their bark canoes the two miles between the Fox and the Wisconsin Rivers in 1673, on their way to discover the Mississippi. In his reading, Turner followed in the footsteps of the French voyageurs who had paddled up the rivers and hacked out the first portages through the woods of Wisconsin. Jean Nicolet, the first white man to set foot in Wisconsin, wore a magnificent damask robe and carried "thunder in both hands." When the Winnebago saw him they declared that he must be the Manitouiriniou, the Wonderful Man.

As a boy, it had astonished Turner to hear Indians, passing a certain place, a bend in the river or a particular tree, quite naturally mutter a greeting to the ancestor place.

These Indians could actually hear their murmuring voices, like the trees in Dante's poem, see the invisible people walking among the trees, the faces floating up from the floor of consciousness. Pierre Esprit Radisson had found in these forests, "dark as in a cellar . . . a labyrinth of pleasure" and regretted that "ye world could not discover such enticing countrys to live in."

For several months more the young Turner was confined to bed with his illness. He loved to stare at the marbled end-papers of his books, which had a hypnotic effect on him. As he sat and pored over his atlas, the maps were dream lakes flowing into each other. In that solitary year he yearned that he might become the poet of the frontier.

Turner at thirty still shared some characteristics with the boy who, home for a year, had dreamed so assiduously. The hero he had imagined himself to be in those private moments was not quite the genial gentleman "Fred Turner" appeared to be to his contemporaries. He yearned to achieve greatness; by 1892, he had an inkling that it might come by his writing a "frontier theory."

For an intellectual career, the University of Wisconsin was perhaps not the most conspicuous choice. However, Turner was nothing if not ambitious. In addition to his research and his teaching load at the university, he had that winter undertaken an arduous series of "extension lectures" in remote towns. These extension lectures were "the Wisconsin idea": it was the motto of the university that "the boundaries of the campus are the boundaries of the State." What pleased his audiences in these lectures were simple and lively stories of the making of the West, which made no demand on the intellect. These lectures were delivered with more emphasis on rhetoric than on substance. He told his uneducated audiences what they wanted to hear. Not for them the complexities of multiple causation and the reliability of evidence. They wanted to hear his message, plain and clear: that the frontier was important, and that they themselves, their ordinary struggling lives, were crucial to the creation of America. For each of these extension lectures, Turner was paid by the University of Wisconsin a fee of ten dollars, plus expenses. He stayed in inns and hotels, rooms above rough saloons; or he was billeted with families in towns too small to have hotels. On many occasions that winter, Turner traveled all night on the unheated trains, with only his traveling rug for comfort, moving through the dead white world of forty below zero.

Nearly everyone he met was impressed by his demeanor, the modest, charming young professor whose smiling blue eyes seemed to radiate to the other person a message of the fundamental decency of his being—and of his view of the world. Turner had been born and raised in Portage, Wisconsin, only one generation removed from the frontier experience, and his love of the woods and outdoor pursuits, no less than his considered views on the significance of the frontier in American history, were tinged by more than a little of this boyhood innocence.

Turner's idea of heaven, he once wrote to a friend, was "a good fishing camp in some remote part of Paradise where the work of creation is not too far advanced." In his frequent excursions into the wilderness, he lived again in the forest of his Portage childhood: the walks, the fishing with his father, the feeling of walking together joyful and silent through God's golden morning; for a moment, the hidden life of lost Portage continued to shape him. In spite of this confidence, his busy routine of teaching at Madison, as well as his extension lectures, there was still the sick part of himself, a dark place without speech, which was straining all the time, no matter how small the town he found himself in, no matter how shabby the room for the night, straining to overhear the chance remark, listening for the clue, the single word carelessly uttered, which would be for him the beacon, the fire on the road.

The frontier must have its poet; but it seemed that his mind had blunted itself by the summer of 1892, and that nothing but a month of indulging his ardent love of fly-fishing would revive his ambition.

Eager though he was to be off on his fishing trip, he was kept in Madison a week longer than he had intended by the arrival of his second child, Jackson Allen, on June 26. His daughter, Dorothy, was nearly two. Mae and the new baby were both well, but Turner was also delayed by various petty academic matters. He had agreed to give a lecture to the Contemporary Club on "Romance and Reality in the Frontier." He returned year after year to Balsam Point, and what he sought there was "the first place," the primeval forests and sunlit lakes of all those years before.

In the morning Turner set off alone with his rucksack and fly-rod case and followed the "Wazee" trail, which in the Winnebago language means "tall pine," until he came to the river. He stood looking down into the swirling water. The current ran fast over the rocks. Further along, he saw that there were logging booms on the river, and the water

had a brown, inky look. On the riverbanks were deadheads, logs which had escaped the booms and become
heavy with water. There would be no fishing in that part of
the river.

Turner looked across at the blackened hillside of the
slashing, the charred stumps and the rotten logs washed up
on the riverbanks. The leaves of the birch trees were shimmering with heat. There was a tinge of burning in the air,
maybe from loggers, or from the Indian mission further
along the shore. The wind carried up from the lake the
sounds of Indian girls bathing. He could hear clearly the
noises they made in their play, splashing the water, their
whoops and shrieks of laughter. The distant sound of the
paddlewheel beating the water was at once puzzling and
familiar.

He sensed something in the trees, as if someone were
hiding in the shadows. Such was his feeling of alarm that
several times he stopped and looked back, expecting to see
Indians moving soundlessly along the trail behind him.
From somewhere in the forest he heard the clean sharp
cracks of an axe splitting wood. Then everything went very
quiet in the woods. There was a parting through the grass,
now moving slowly in the morning breeze. The ground
was not trampled, but the way the grass swayed in the air
like that gave him the feeling that someone had just passed
that way.

From there he followed other, older trails, scarcely distinguishable from the forest floor. He walked through balsam trees, sugar maple, swamp lilies, and goldenrod. When
he had first gone into Temple Woods that morning there
were still patches of snow clinging to the rocks like ghostly

moss. The trunks of trees were like the texture of stone. From somewhere came the sound of running water. This place seemed to belong to a different botanical region. The shadows ahead of him moved along the forest floor among the ferns and bright lichens, dark ivy.

He entered a place where the hemlock firs and pines grew close together, shutting out the light. It was a mighty place, a place of ancestors, of voices creaking in the mossy trees. It was an eerie sensation, walking there in the deep shadow of the trees, the voice murmuring through the trees, as though the dark itself were speaking. As he walked, his feet were soundless on the bed of pine needles, striped in bars of amber sunlight. It was as though no foot-step could be heard in the presence of this greater silence. Then, somewhere off in the darkness of the trees he heard a rainbird call, and he heard the voices of the hemlocks creaking, as though in answer to the birdcall.

When he heard the voice, it made his heart beat quick. He stood there for a long time with his head cocked, listen-ing. The voice was muffled and indistinct, as sometimes the wind will carry from a neighbor's house snatches of conver-sation that seem to make no sense. At first he thought it might have been Indians using their own language, but the voice was even lighter, something spectral, like a breath.

It was a voice which began in the trees, then followed him through the secret forest paths, and rushed along the Wazee trail like a wind. It was dark, voiceless speech. There were words in it, but he could not quite make them out. The words were sung, like a hymn; there was a new note in the voice of the woods, like a voice raised up to God, part praising, part beseeching. It reminded him of the sound of his own voice as a little child, saying his prayers. He felt it in himself, as well as in the air: the feeling of a breath being gently exhaled.

He felt that same moment of creamy strangeness which precedes sex, that transition between when one realizes that sexual intercourse is going to take place and the first penetration, the exquisite resistance of yielding flesh. From the trees behind him, all was stillness, a world patiently waiting for its time.

He came upon the old ceremonial place where cone-shaped stones, brightly patterned, had been laid out in clusters on the ground. They were painted yellow, blue and brown. He thought they might have been old Indian fire stones, but a few more steps and he came across different shapes and patterns. In some of these stones holes had been drilled and shafts fitted. Some of the smooth stones had been painted with the pictograph for sorrow, an eye with teardrops falling from it. Some were circumcised, and looked like mushroom caps; others were spiraled, like corkscrews. Some stones had been fashioned at one end into handles, and looked like rattles. The next group of stones had been painted with ocher. On the ground were many clamshells. Somewhere off in the trees, he heard the plover call again.

He could see the surface of the lake glittering through the trees. He heard the drone of insects in the shadows at the edge of the water. He sat down, his back resting against the trunk of a big cedar. His head was level with the bars of dusty sunlight, which seemed to have the aromatic cedar smell. The quiet waters of the lake spread before him; as he watched, ripples reached the reflections of the trees and made them wobble. The trees above him seemed immense, and when he looked up at them, he felt that his head and limbs were made of heavy stone. He closed his eyes and listened to the sound of insects.

When next he looked, a figure had entered the lake and begun to swim, each stroke barely rippling the skin of the water. Her hair streamed out behind her. Then she had risen from the lake and stood there in the shallows. The light coming off the surface of the lake was so bright it hurt his eyes, like a fine mist of rain.

The Indian girl seemed to come from a long way off, from a place where it was always night. Although he did not understand it, he felt that she rose from a perfectly still and pitiless point in his own being. Tears filled his eyes. His stern look softened, the whole look of his face was transformed. The figure of the girl drew not just words but the very secrets from his heart. She made him feel so full of pain and longing, he felt that this was what it must be like to go mad.

He felt the forest close around him, an encroaching dark. The vision lingered as though on the point of dissolving, her skin the color of tobacco, standing there in the shallow waters of the lake among the salt-dead trees, three feet of iodine-colored water lapping her legs. In her dark eyes there was a look of faint puzzlement, as though she might have recognized him from some time in the past. When he looked again, she was gone. There was no human presence, just the wobbling reflections of trees risen again in the mirror of the lake.

———

Late in the afternoon Turner walked back to the inn at Balsam Point, where he stored his catch in the ice shed. It was his habit then to sit for a while in the bar and drink a glass of whiskey, before eating his supper and retiring early to his room. One evening he was engaged in conversation by a man named Robertson. He asked Robertson where the fishing was good this year. The other man replied that he was not the best person to ask, as he came from Chicago, but he believed there were still good places upriver, away from the trail, in Temple Woods, where loggers had not yet reached. Though Turner was still listening to this Robertson, he felt himself drift a long way off, so that after a while the sound of the other man's voice brought him back with a jolt. "Why should a woman who has lived in palaces and dined with kings, if we are to believe her tales, be living in a place like this?" He realized Robertson must have been talking about the lady who had just entered the inn and crossed the room to the telegraph desk. Men's eyes followed the movement of her bustle.

Pauline L'Allemand was conspicuous with her Chicago dresses, her red hair and arrogant eyes; as was her son, Edgar, with his bowtie and blue silk waistcoat, the way he limped along behind her with his telescope and aluminum violin. She apparently had been a famous opera singer in Europe, but at Balsam Point it had already been decided that Pauline was a witch. "They say she hears things," Robertson confided. "They say she hears speech in the woods."

"What?" Turner demanded.

"That's what they do up there at the old house in the trees, her and the photographer. Trying to make photographs of the spirits. Have you heard of the Theosophical Society? I don't mind telling you that they have aroused quite a bit of local interest. It's the disappearances, you know. The lost girls."

Robertson seemed to know a lot about it. In fact he seemed unusually well informed, and even listed the names of the girls from around there who had disappeared without trace over the past few summers—Carolyn Tozier, Jessie Olsen, Fern Perry, Sadie Kind, Memmie Reinholt. "They say she hears speech in the woods," he repeated. "She's in touch with a spirit. But the local folk here say it's no mystery. It's just a girl that took strychnine over at the Indian camp years ago. They say they heard her screams all night across the lake."

"Took strychnine, you say? In God's name, why?"

"It don't bear thinking about what people will do."

"I guess it don't." The conversation had taken a distasteful direction and Turner tried to disengage himself.

"It's an evil thing, right enough," Robertson said. "Usually there's just one reason."

Turner had spent another day fishing. He packed his catch in his rucksack, stored his fly-rod in its case and set off home down the trail through a stand of birches. Although there was no wind, the leaves on the low branches moved nervously, like a trembling hand. The trail became two wheel ruts in the grass. It was the old logging road. He heard the nervous sound of horses somewhere in the trees. The meeting of sunny, leafy trees overhead was like a tunnel of green light. It felt like the light was drawing him through the trees.

As he was walking along the logging road, a horse and cart passed him, headed back toward the inn. He stepped aside to let the wagon pass, two horses, four wheels, springs jigging under the load of wood. Tom Whitecloud and his squaw sat up there, wearing blankets. As they passed, the Indian touched his hat. The smell of the Indians was like the smell of salmon rotting in a dry riverbed in winter.

A mile from Balsam Point was the last of the summer places. From somewhere inside the house came a musical phrase on a violin, developed, ceased, then repeated again. The sun threw the shadows of trees across the front of the house in violent stripes.

Along one side of the path was a row of tall stakes to which raspberry canes had been tied with lengths of stocking. The sweet smell of apples wafted from the orchard. A cider press stood rusting among the weeds. A boy was at work at the side of the house. He looked Mongol, as though the hand that had made his face had pinched the eye sockets together.

Turner heard the phrase of music again. This time the phantom musician continued with the piece. The notes of the violin seemed to weave the bright air around him, to draw him toward the dark porch with its ox-yoke lintel. Turner made himself walk on toward Balsam Point through the poison oak and ivy.

———

Turner sometimes saw Billy Sunday, the boy from the house, digging for worms under the mulch of pine needles near the shore of the lake. Not for him the fancy sport of fly-fishing: he sprinkled cornmeal on the surface to get the lake trout to rise and baited his hooks with worms, perch eyes or goldenrod galls. Turner would see him on the porch of the inn, or sitting on the dock reading the Bible he kept in his leather satchel. Turner felt sorry for this poor farm boy with his suffering face. Turner wondered what had happened to him in his young life to have given him such a look of anguish. But there was something else. Although he had never seen the boy before his arrival here this summer, Turner felt he recognized his face from somewhere.

The photographer and the opera singer left the house together in the mornings with their cameras. Turner saw the square black wagon travel down the old logging road, the skeins of fog still hanging in the silver birches. The photographer wore a starched collar and cuffs, a black jacket and trousers, and shoes which had been polished to a high shine. He was hatless, and his hair was combed neatly with a part in the middle. It seemed that they were still conducting their experiments in spirit photography.

Turner walked along the railroad track, a branch of the Soo Line, which divided the solid world of forest rising high on either side. He left the Soo Line and made his way along a logging road through some second-growth pine, a corner of the great forest that had been logged out. The road led to a blackened slashing where loggers had been. They had been using heavy horses in there, hauling the piles of logs cut the previous summer and lost under the snow during the winter. There were still deep wheel ruts in the damp black ground from the heavy carts.

The afternoon was hot, but the branches overhead kept the stream in shadow. He was lost in his own world, the sound of the stream around the tops of his waders, the shadows moving along the forest floor among the lichens and ferns, dark ivy. He saw the flashing of a trout in the sandy bottom of the stream. He cast his fly carefully on the surface of the pool. The water moved at the tops of his waders. At his back the line of trout was tied between the trees. Big green-black flies were buzzing around the trout. There was no sound except for the flies near the line of fish. Then he heard from somewhere a sound like oars creaking. Then a light echo, concentrated, coiled, rifling through the trees: the sound of a twig being snapped underfoot.

He went over and placed his rod carefully next to the rucksack. He took off his waders and, in spite of the heat, wrapped his old mackinaw blanket around him and lay back against the trunk of the tree. Holding his head to one side, he listened intently, as though waiting for someone.

Turner followed the Indian girl along the forest floor, which was softer and damper here, and the tree roots above the ground were like the shapes of contorted limbs. Those shapes were like bones exposed in the earth of an old graveyard. The big damp lichen-covered shapes pushed up into the fresh world, corrupting the spicy cedar smell of the air.

A little further on, she stopped and, leaning forward

against the trunk of a cedar pine to keep her balance, she lifted her left foot and began rubbing it with the fingers of her right hand. Perhaps she had trodden on a thorn, for she remained in that position for a minute or so, rubbing the sole of her foot. For an uncomfortable moment their eyes met, and he quickly looked away.

There was the strong smell of mud from the lake. The very air he breathed seemed to have been sweated up from the dark earth. From the unseen lake came the chugging of the wood-burning steamer, *The Lady of the Lake*. Human voices rose, fell and were lost in the great trees beyond the darkening lake. The girls were returning from Temple Woods. Their voices died in the air, as if they were under heavy snow. There was a noise nearby, like a sudden intake of air, followed by a rapid easy beating. Somewhere nearby the swan rose from the water and ascended.

The Indian girl kept looking at him as she always did, every time they met, with an expression of such intensity that he now began to suspect it might be hate. When he felt her eyes on him, a hand passed over his spine, making his skin prickle. She opened the front of her red shirt and he felt himself sinking to his knees, unwilling to go on, but he was caught on a hook now, and he felt her dragging him on, deeper into the trees. It was as though there were a hook which would not allow him to withdraw his gaze from her.

He felt the blood come to his face. His heart had begun to pound, racing ahead of the consequences. Turner heard his own voice pleading, "What do you want from me? Every day I feel you watching me, I feel your eyes on me, wanting something of me." She stared at him, and when Turner tried to speak again, she placed a brown hand over his mouth. "Come. I taste like fish," she said. "I taste like the sea." She spread the red shirt on the ground. She lay back and opened her legs and he felt the net in his abdomen tighten. His excitement was like aching, like pain, the slow curling movement of a living creature inside his body.

He went down between her legs and kissed her other, salty mouth. That mouth was a darker color than the rest of her skin, and the black line which ran all the way around her lips down there was the same line that traced her irises. They lay then with their faces close, eyes open in the deep shade. He could not take his eyes away from hers. Her skin seemed to soak in the darkness of the woods and became the same indigo color of her tattoo.

He felt the friction and resistance of her skin, then the sudden rubbery movement as her body gave way and he slipped into her. A whimper escaped her, in protest or in pain; but the strange thing was that she held him all the more tightly with her legs, and he feared he might explode as soon as he was inside her.

Every time he returned here to the lakeside and forced himself into her, she made a whimpering noise and drew breath, as though she were upset about something. Her breath came out sudden and loud, but her face was still perfectly composed, a calm sculpted mask.

He felt the force of her desire. The distressed sound of her breathing excited him, as though she were struggling for breath, and the smell again, the salt and fish smell of the shallow brown lake on a humid day, with a warm wind, just before a storm.

She lowered herself onto him and rode him in the airless gloom as the smell of the wildflowers crept around them.

For some reason, the fact that it was daylight seemed to him unbearably sad. All that afternoon he could feel the sadness of the daylight and the sad smell of the hidden flowers.

He felt her sinking down in the lake. He was caught on a hook between her legs. She was dragging him down. Then he felt her dragging him up to the surface. He dived again, but he could not extract himself from her cavity. He tried to pull it out, but each time some mysterious power drew it urgently back in again.

A plantation of rubbery trees was growing through his sinew, even now threatening to break through the surface of his skin. The soft roots of the trees were writhing down through his stomach and into the muscles of his thighs. He felt crows feeding on him on a vast dry plain, dream trees shimmering on the horizon. Weird birds, tall as men, stood on two legs behind him and lightly pecked their beaks into his back. A needle of sunny peace was moving gently down through the knuckles of his spine, and he felt the creamy feeling float up through his belly.

Suddenly she stopped and wanted to do it the other way. Astern, she called it. She knelt and pointed her spine straight at his heart. She let out a scream. He had missed the place she wanted and instead of pleasure he had filled her with hot wounding pain. "That hurts," she said. Even as he was rhythmically forcing his flesh inside hers, he could think of nothing but the sound she made, as though she were struggling for breath. "That's it. Right against my bone," she said. Every time she drew a breath, her whole body seemed to heave, and she made a whimpering noise.

He felt the warm beast smile in his blood. All the savagery was gone now. A new feeling of lightness and tenderness was flowing up through his limbs, and he heard a voice come as if from a long way away and penetrate the cushion of warmth around his face. She said, "Come on. I want you to shoot."

There was the smell of feces on her, gritted deep into the weave of her skin. She smelled like freshly turned earth. She had been shaped by the worship of his hands, like a clay statue. A slight creaking noise caught his attention. At first he feared it might have been someone hiding in the trees, watching him; maybe Billy Sunday. But it was not so much the sound of a movement as something lighter, metaphysical, a momentary realignment in the scheme of things, the shifting of the weight of the world from one foot to the other.

He felt the needle move gently up his spine, then plunge into his head, killing thought, and he relaxed. In the scorching winds, in the frozen snowdrifts that followed, he tried to forget who this other person was. Their skin was still touching, but he felt suddenly very separate from her. He closed his eyes tightly, but when he opened them again, she was still there. Lights pulsed at the edges of his vision. She heaved for breath, there were drops of sweat on her forehead and upper lip, and she was moaning, as though she were ill.

Desire had passed along the rails of time into an unknown country. The moment he had been filled with pleasure and had closed his eyes, another scene entirely was playing before him, as if on a magic lantern. Somewhere in the night a circus passed through the dreaming forest. He could hear the locomotive, the sounds of the elephants trumpeting in the hour before dawn, the balsam trees shaking out their fabulous ovation.

But now from the trees all was stillness. It no longer felt like a real place, subject to the physical laws of wind and sun and rain. It was like a place that had been cast outside the laws of nature. The silence spread around the two figures on the forest floor, a quietness not of sleeping, but a state of deathliness right down deep inside themselves.

Turner was walking home to the inn along the logging road in the bitter, grass-stained light of dusk. He felt exhausted. He was looking forward to being alone in his attic room with his bottle, anticipating that fuzzy acceptance of all things that is the purpose of whiskey. The notes of a piano drifted through the trees as clear and sharp as the tinkle of glasses. He heard a woman singing, her voice rising and falling on the evening breeze, soothing and intimate.

He approached the house, hoping to catch a glimpse through a window. He was aware of the impropriety, the danger of his situation. What if he should be discovered lurking there in his dirty mackinaw, with his trout rod in his hand, and an accusation should be made against him? He wanted simply to turn and walk away, go up to his attic room at the inn and be rid of this feeling.

Yet he was immobilized. Once he had gone into an unsavory hotel in the Negro district in Chicago and had stood there, struck dumb, unable to move forward or backward in just this way.

The strange thing was that he took a kind of pleasure in

it. For a while now the singing and the piano had stopped. Turner continued to lurk like a thief in the porch, which had been screened against mosquitoes. Then, without allowing himself time for further indecision, he knocked.

There came the sound of a heavy boot and brace limping down the passage. Edgar, who was in evening dress, said, "Splendid!" as though Turner standing there in his fishing clothes was exactly what he expected to find.

There had been times during the days when Turner had suddenly stopped moving, certain he was being watched. He had seen Edgar in his silk hat in the tower of the house holding a telescope to his eye, surveying the world of the dark trees. Edgar spent a lot of time watching from the tower. And he had passed Edgar on the logging road to Balsam Point, holding his shotgun by its hexagonal barrel, stock resting over his shoulder. Edgar walked slowly because of his brace.

The passage was dark, and the rooms they passed were dark, too, as though the encroaching forest had blocked out all the light. From under the door at the end of the passage came a thin blade of lamplight.

The lady was standing before a music stand wearing a stage dress of shimmering pleated silk. She looked up at her visitor, recognizing him from the inn, or from the road past the house. She said, "Of course. You heard me singing." But she too seemed to be expecting him.

It was an unusual room, self-consciously Bohemian, quite out of place in a logging town. There was a red lacquer screen in the Japanese style, and lengths of gauzy material hung from the ceiling. There were photographs on the walls, like a gallery, bathing photographs of women, studies in classical poses in nature. He had heard that in certain circles it was the done thing for women to have an album of nude studies of their female friends. In that room there was a peculiar smell, the flour-and-water smell of semen.

On a table next to the window was a large bronze Buddha, three feet tall, on a pedestal with columns on the side, like a wise physician looking down at his patient. Beside the statue there were books and papers, musical manuscripts. But there was also an Indian artifact, a barbarous thing, a gorget made from a human scalp, engraved and decorated with blue birds.

The lady moved in front of the large gilt mirror over the fireplace. She let down her hair and slowly began to brush it. Her face was flushed. The young man said, "Mother's skin can't bear the least rays of the sun. The least bit of sun and she breaks out. Red-headed people can't take the sun too much." Edgar continued to regard him with his frank, friendly gaze.

She said, "You'll be meeting our Mr. Van Schaick. He is a quite remarkable person. He is tired just now. We have been in the woods all day, taking pictures. We are conducting some experiments in spirit photography. Have you heard of the Theosophical Society? I don't mind telling you that we have produced some remarkable results."

Turner said, "I believe you were an opera singer in Germany. Is that where you are from?"

Pauline had turned to the mirror to brush her hair. She said, "I went to Germany to study singing as a girl. Actually, I grew up in Syracuse, New York, the only daughter of Irma Elhasser, a poor dressmaker. I was born in 1862 and I can't remember ever seeing my father, though I have a picture of him in his Union uniform, holding me in his arms. I had a lonely childhood, but so did many others in those days. After the Civil War, we were a nation without fathers."

Turner stared at Pauline in the mirror. The brush stroked through her long hair, the glossy color of deer, foxes, red hens. She said to Turner, "Of course, you are still waiting to hear me sing." A slight smile played at the corners of her mouth.

The young dandy took his place at the piano and began to play. Pauline opened her mouth wide and Turner was astonished by the pure, shocking stream of sound that poured out. A flush extended along her throat and into the reddened skin above her breasts and she had a distressed look on her face. She held the note, fierce and steady, her eyes unnaturally wide, and as the pitch of her voice intensified, the room seemed to take on the golden color of her voice.

She took in breath, and the passion of her voice made the flesh of her upper arms shake. Turner recognized the aria from *Don Giovanni*. The vengeful ghost of the Commendatore had risen from his grave. Recognizing the aria made Turner feel tolerant, cosmopolitan, like a man who has recently broadened his horizons. But then her voice began to affect him in a different way. Each note, each word was drawing him in more tightly. The mood of the music had infected him, colored his thoughts, darkened his spirits. She was singing the music of guilt.

Gradually, eerily, Turner became aware that there was someone else in the room. The soaring, dreamlike voice brought back the Indian girl's black hair, the dark eyes which had looked at him with such meaning. The intensity of the moment was almost unbearable. The girl's lithe young form floated in the lamplight near the window for a little longer, then vanished.

Turner realized that Pauline had finished singing some time ago now. He suddenly feared he had betrayed himself, and that Pauline or Edgar might have been able to see into his most private exultation.

But there was someone else who was part of the scene, of the room but not in it. Someone was standing just outside the open window. Turner saw it was the stable boy, that solitary, unhappy-looking creature. Billy Sunday stood there, an outcast from the warm comforting light inside the house. What struck Turner was the intensely serious way Billy Sunday was gazing through the window at the place where the Indian girl had appeared. His face was full of light, full of wonder. Then the boy was kneeling on the ground out there, hands clasped in an attitude of prayer.

Turner felt tainted by a kind of complicity. He noticed how much his behavior now had become furtive, had begun to resemble that of one who had committed a crime. Simply by witnessing the boy kneeling in front of the lighted window, Turner remembered for a long time afterward that look of wonder, the terrible belief in Billy Sunday's face.

Edgar rose from the piano stool, took a handkerchief and began to dab at his forehead, which glistened with perspiration. Seeing the boy outside now, Edgar called to him, "That voice of hers. Have you ever heard anything like it, Billy Sunday? She can break windows with it. Another Mary Ricks." He laughed loudly and said, "You know, Mary Ricks, the Wisconsin Window Smasher?"

But Billy Sunday did not hear him. He continued to gaze up into the room, at where the girl had stood, when Pauline had opened her mouth and that first shocking sound had come out.

Turner's sleep was disturbed that night by a thunderstorm. At one point he woke to see lightning branch across the sky. He felt the whole building shake, heard the hiss of plaster dust falling from the ceiling and walls, and another sound, as though the claws of lightning had sizzled into the surface of the lake, as when a blacksmith plunges a glowing horseshoe into a pail of water. Turner lay on his mattress, sweating, awake. The sky was divided, the line of a shore. Half the sky was night-blue, containing the moon; to the north was the solid shoreline of black sky, broken only at the edge by swirling, lighter-colored clouds. The great waves of the thunder rumbled away in organ chords across the lake. In that unreal state of mind between dreaming and waking, the thunder seemed to come from the wall of trees, as though the mighty noise originated not in the sky but in a river rumbling deep under the dark earth.

Outside his window the branches of the trees began to shiver like birds, then to sway, and the wind brought sprays of rain. The mad sky seemed to be boiling down upon him. He could hear the wind in the forest breaking the trees. The storm was like some dark thing stalking its prey, a black furious energy so close his whole body tensed in fright. It was like something on the landing, hurling its full weight against his door.

But there was also another presence in the night. When next the moon shocked the night world into white being, a figure was standing in the dark of his room, not tall, but lithe and muscular. Something about its shape seemed almost bestial. She wore a cloak of owl feathers, caked with mud and leaves, streaked with blood. Her face was so white it was as though the color had been bleached out of it. It was a ghostly mask, the bewitched clay Winnebago face he had seen so many times in the trees.

The darkness crept around her again, took over her shape, until she was hardly there at all, a shadow, a darkness in the mirror. "Jane?" he said. "Jane?" As he stared at her in the mirror, the skin of her face grew cloudy, her body became smoke. She seemed to hang in the air in front of him for a moment longer, then disappeared.

The wind in the trees moved in and whispered to him, flowed through him. The Wisconsin woods closed around him with its visions, its fevers and epidemics, its fear. The sound of rain on the roof was like faint, conspiring applause. He felt his heart leaping out of his chest. He lay awake in his bed, head pulsing, unable to stop trembling. He heard a splashing from out in the lake, a canoe, a phantom arm beating the water, vanishing into the night.

Somehow he would have to get through the long hours which stretched ahead until morning. In those wakeful hours, he crossed the dream line and was back in Temple Woods again, the tree trunks closing in around him. He wandered again among the black shining trees, and felt the old furtive excitement. These hemlock woods were an ancestor place, a quiet and dead world, a world of secrets. He felt her presence, like something bruising the air, and he felt himself being taken over by the silence of Temple Woods, drawn further and further into the trees.

In his dream state he heard her quiet sobbing in the trees, a sound whose echo pursues men all their lives, a sadness which they silently pass on to their wives and children, even when the occasion itself, the woman's face and name are all forgotten, even when the men are middle-aged and old and dying and all that is left is the moment of uncertainty, the vague, nauseous feeling that the way of the world is always like this and all we can do, finally, is go to sleep.

And now he could hear a chugging sound, steady and rhythmic, like a train. The sound became the chugging of *The Lady of the Lake* on her way from the Indian mission. He heard the elephant shriek of its steam whistle as it approached Balsam Point. The weekly mail boat was back. He would leave in the morning.

He lay and listened to the chugging of *The Lady of the Lake*, the scraps of human voices flung on the wind, those faint murmurs from the world beyond his own, from the Indian camp on the other side of the lake. The night breeze across the surface of the lake carried the dreamlike sounds of the night, trumpeting circus elephants, a sound like a girl screaming.

Early the next morning Turner packed his rucksack and fly-rod case and put on his mackinaw in order to leave. Downstairs he had breakfast and asked to settle up for his room.

"You leaving?" the clerk asked.

"That's right."

"You're not leaving. Listen. The black diphtheria has broken out at the Indian mission. It is affecting the Chippewa papooses very badly." It seemed that a notice of quarantine had been issued. All services on *The Lady of the Lake* had been suspended.

A plump man in shirtsleeves came onto the dock and approached the lone figure at the end. It was Robertson, the man who had spoken to Turner at the inn earlier in the week. "Were you trying to leave too?" he asked. "The rats always desert a sinking ship." His belly was tight in his shirt and he was red-faced. Robertson lifted his face and smiled and the sunlight caught the shiny whiskers on the points of his cheekbones. "You must have a good catch stored in that ice shed by now."

"I don't care."

"Ah. And I had taken you for a genuine sportsman."

Robertson began to talk about the epidemic. More of the Indians were going down with the diphtheria every day, he said. Several had already died. Last night in the storm a few of them had broken quarantine and crossed the water in their canoes. They were locked in jail for the night and, now, back to the Indian camp with them. Robertson winked. "You are talking to the law, you know!" He informed Turner that he was an assistant superintendent with Pinkerton's Detective Agency in Chicago.

The wind lifted on the surface of the lake and the sound of hammering came from *The Lady of the Lake*. A man appeared on the deck. "See that? That's Tom Thunder, the tracker," Robertson said.

The man's long black hair hung straight down at the sides of his carved-wood face. He wore a blue woolen vest and the bottom half of pyjamas tucked into his unlaced boots. The skin on his face followed the ridges of muscle and bone underneath. He stood in silence on the deck, staring with concentration across the lake. There was no change in that face of carved wood.

There were other Indians squatting in the shade on the dock with soiled rags wrapped around them. They were too weak to walk, and when they moved, they dragged themselves along like animals with broken hind legs, their eyes averted. One of them, a young squaw, slowly made her way along the dock toward them. Her ribcage moved in quick shallow movements and she made a curious noise as she advanced, a kind of croaking. When she was close to them, her head slowly lifted. There was a look in her eyes as though she had seen something which utterly terrified her. There were black patches on her legs, as though her skin had been stained by smoke. From somewhere Turner heard the sound of dogs barking.

"She's going bad," said Robertson. "Lord, she do smell bad."

"For God's sake," said Turner. "Where is the doctor?"

"The doctor has gone away."

"When will he be returning?"

"The doctor will not be returning."

All the time now Turner heard the faint baying of dogs a long way off, somewhere in the woods. The woman on the dock in front of them moaned again.

"You'd better keep away from her," Robertson said. "They are diseased. Disease is retribution. Isn't that what the Bible tells us?"

"When will a doctor be available?" Turner asked.

"A doctor will not be available."

The sound of the dogs baying echoed across the lake. Turner tried to remember where he was, why the sound seemed so close. Robertson said that another girl had disappeared. Twyla Flake had been gone three days now. Someone had claimed she had run away, as so many girls do, with a showman from the Ringling Brothers Circus and they had been hiding in Temple Woods. Now they were looking for her.

There was no feeling in Turner's legs. His whole body had gone numb. He felt he was stuck in thick mud. It was dangerous to inquire too much. He tried to judge how close those dogs were, on the other side of the lake. He was shivering again, and now he started to shake more violently, as though it were his own blood those hounds were baying for.

3

BILLY SUNDAY

If he had dreamed of the circus train already, it must be morning. But it was still dark, no rooster, nor other birds. There came the sound from yesterday in the forest. The night air moved and the train came hammering closer, then fell away again, became a pattern of rising and falling. First close, then far away again. On it goes, now near, now further, the thumping of the locomotive, the creaking of the carriages of the circus train swaying around the bend in the tracks. Then Billy Sunday heard, much closer, in the stable on the other side of the barn wall, above the shifting of hooves and the creaking of a leather harness, the sound of hammering.

He lay in the red barn with the smell of ripe corn and dry soil in the summer night. The hall clock inside the house had begun striking and he had forgotten to count . . . four, five, then stops. To think back before he was counting: how many? Did he start counting before the first one without knowing it, or had there been more? He thought back to whether he had heard the mechanical whirring before it strikes. Yes. Only five. But if it was only five o'clock in the morning, before the sun had risen, why had he dreamed of the circus train and woken? And why, now, could he still hear it?

Then he must have slept, for when he heard the clock inside the house strike again, he counted from the whirring before the first chime. Seven. And somehow the barn had grown full of light. A skin of summer dew lay on the window. As he opened the window, his thoughts were still back in his dream of the circus train, the open car carrying the band wagon decorated with golden winged angels, a beautiful girl's carved face, and the Stars and Stripes painted on the side.

It was then Billy Sunday saw the signs of death in the farmyard. Something had got into the chicken coop. The disemboweled carcasses, the chickens with their heads bitten off were everywhere. He thought of a sudden hawk dropping from the sky and piercing their necks with sharp claws. Now he saw the glossy red hen that had been nailed to the barn door. He looked at the rough-adzed boards with their deep scars, and wondered what could have made savage marks like that.

And Billy Sunday gave this day a name. He called it Enemy.

———

Then at midmorning it began to be night again. The sky grew dark and the sun died. It began to rain very quietly. The house settled, gutters began to creak. He stayed indoors. There would be no work that day.

Billy Sunday listened to the rain on the roof of the barn. Once, he heard the windmill at the well turn its face for no reason, a rusty bray of pain. Inside the barn was dark. The sepia-dark air seemed filled with someone else.

A locomotive had passed through the forest. Later, when he climbed the tower and looked through Edgar's telescope across the bay to the railroad track, he could not see the circus train. The circus had gone away. Billy Sunday heard again, beyond that room in the barn, the thumping of the engine, the trumpeting of elephants. That dreaming moment before dawn when he had heard the circus train stayed with Billy Sunday. He could still hear, beyond the comforting aura of Copenhagen tobacco, the clanking of the engine, the distressed sounds the animals were making, that fleeting menagerie in the hour before dawn.

He lay on the grey blankets with the puzzle of it pressing down on him.

The cider was kept in big earthenware jugs in a disused wash house in the back of the barn, which Mr. Van Schaick had set up as a temporary studio, and it was there, as he went that rainy afternoon to steal some cider, that Billy Sunday found the stack of glass plates, thirty in all, the results of Van Schaick's and Pauline's experiments in spirit photography.

Billy Sunday looked at the heavy glass plates. It might

have been his own failure to mix thoroughly the silver nitrate emulsion, or the failed results of the photographer's experiments in creating certain effects by the double exposure of the plates to light, that had caused these spectral presences to leak like dark stains across the glass plates. Vague forms of men and women seemed to be moving through the trees, indistinct figures, clothed in fuzzy auras of light.

The members of the Theosophical Society had assembled in their white skirts and black blouses. They were all hatless among the trees, and on the negative plates their faces looked dark as Negroes. The ladies were dressed as for a Sunday School picnic rather than as a group of ghoulish midwesterners about to participate in a psychic experiment. The dark faces looked back at him with their stern and puzzled frowns, eyes slitted by the morning sun, dressed in their pinafores, some with false lace collars over their dresses, their white hair like spun sugar.

Billy Sunday could not make it out exactly, but the strange thing was that one of those ghostly figures was naked. The torso, half turned away from the camera's scrutiny, melted into the forest, suffused with light. It was a muscular back, but one which Billy Sunday saw belonged to a woman, or a girl.

He took up the next plate. It was not an anonymous body this time, but a face. The subject had not been part of the ritual of the cambric handkerchief. This face was different from the others. It was the color of her skin. On the glass plate's negative image, the girl's face and hair were so white. She seemed to be too white. Her skin was the color of frost.

Billy Sunday did not know exactly why he began to make his own prints from this plate, in the dank-smelling wash house, that afternoon, but in doing so he was aware that he had entered another world. The shapes on the glass plates came from the forest floor, the matted vegetation, dark and soft, the tortured branches in Temple Woods arrested in movement, writhing in the air.

Billy Sunday's hands trembled as he printed the photograph. The betrayal of his employer's trust was only part of the cause of his agitation. As she swam toward him through the solution in the printing tray, her face was not white, but dark. In the photographic print, the face had a slightly blurred appearance, her high forehead otherworldly. She was the tobacco-skinned girl he had seen in Temple Woods.

Her face is like a dream, a fragment carried into the world from sleep. But the dream has needles, piercing his chest. He thought about the cries he had heard so often from the hemlock forest that summer. She cries out, but her cries die in the dark world of the trees.

He busied himself with the tasks of the evening, returning from time to time to his table to look again at the photograph. Mr. Van Schaick had often told him that the camera is "an instrument of God" and that photography reveals the hand of destiny. Perhaps it was the same hand which had left its print on the frosted white flesh of the girl in the glass plate, the "spirit photograph"? The eyes of that girl stared back at him impassively from the photograph, offering no answer.

That trunk also contained the glass plate negatives of Van Schaick's "anthropological" photographs of Indians. Several squaws were sitting in front of the opening of a tent. Their bodies were big shapes, and they were sick, by the look of them. There on the next print, which had been taken closer, he could see the lumpy skin of one of the women, the face ravaged by smallpox. It seemed to Billy Sunday that much the kinder thing to do would have been to put them out of their misery, to aim a rifle at them instead of a camera.

Billy Sunday returned the photographs and glass plates to the trunk. As he moved them, something fell from the bottom of the pile. It was a *carte de visite*, with a lady's photograph. He saw it was a bathing photograph of Pauline, which had been trimmed and mounted on a card two and a half by four inches. Billy Sunday suddenly stood very still, his senses alert. He was accustomed to the photographs in which women wore nothing but a cambric handkerchief over their faces. But he had been shocked when *she* had opened the front of her gown by her white belly and her black pubic patch. She seemed bigger without clothes on, really quite enormous, like the photograph in Van Schaick's studio of Fat Alice from Dallas in the circus. He wasn't sure why it should seem so important. It must have been the smell of the darkroom. Sepia and albumen. Semen and ink.

4

FREDERICK JACKSON TURNER

Turner had not spoken a word to Mr. Van Schaick in all the time since his arrival at Balsam Point. He was surprised, then, when they found themselves alone in the parlor at the inn late one afternoon and they struck up a conversation. Van Schaick was ten years older than Turner. He said he had been born in Rochester, New York, but his family had moved when he was young to a little town in Wisconsin, just fifteen miles from Turner's Portage. The photographer asked him shyly if he would be interested in seeing his collection of Indian artifacts before he took them home to Black River Falls.

His den had been decorated in a simple sporting style, as might be expected in a lodge near the lake, with hunting trophies mounted on the walls and photographs of prize fish. Turner looked around the room. It made a stark contrast with the florid style of the parlor where he had heard Pauline sing. Van Schaick's cameras and other photographic equipment were neatly laid out. On a desk there were piles of photographs and glass plate negatives.

There were also several pamphlets and musical programs on the table. The Wisconsin Spiritualist Union, founded 1870. Black River Falls. Sunday, May 22. Guest artiste: Pauline L'Allemand. Sundry musical items. Afternoon tea. Enquirers' Meeting. 5 P.M. Healing Group. A brochure advertised a free public lecture on "The Sacred Tree of the Winnebago Indians." There were also pamphlets on Living Theosophy, World Unity, and The Key to Knowledge. He wondered if the photographer was really a devotee of Madame Blavatsky or whether he just pretended to go along with Pauline in all this.

He turned his full attention now to the results of Van Schaick's summer's work. Turner had not expected to find such a superb collection. It would not have been out of place in the university museum. There were rock "eggs" painted with pictographs in red ocher, hammer stones with pointed ends, flaked stone arrowheads, a decoy duck made of woven tule bulrushes. There were various lengths of twine and knotted cords; fire sticks; a Manitou pipe carved in the shape of a bird; a sheet of mica cut in the shape of a human hand. There was a feathered cloak and several pairs of moccasins and—something truly remarkable—that gorget made from a human skull, engraved and colored with blue birds.

Turner had seen similar rocks, pictographs of the human

eye with teardrops, piled up in mounds in the clearing in the woods, and he asked the photographer about them.

"Burial mounds," the photographer replied. "They build them where a chief or a princess is buried." He said it as though it was so rudimentary a point that the asker of such a question could hold no more interest for him. Then he added, more sympathetically, "They say it's where the Ghost Dance takes place."

Turner began to look through the photographs of the Indians. The photographer explained that he had been taking these four-by-five-inch snapshots at various times over the past couple of years. In those snapshots the photographer had recorded the shameful secrets of the sick bodies, the smallpox victims lying in the doorways of their tents and squalid cabins. He had captured the drunken women selling themselves among the filth and the stench, the faces lumpy with smallpox. The ridged faces seemed carved from wood, or lumps of clay shaped by hands, darkened with ocher. These photographs were like stains on the human soul, something barbarous, original. As he looked through the photographs of the big shapeless squaws sitting in misery in front of their tents, he saw it in their faces, in their grieving spirits.

The Indian mission was three miles away around the lake shore from the house with the ox-yoke lintel. Turner had ended up there, one afternoon. A group of bark cabins at the lake's edge, rotting into the mud. The first thing he had seen was a pile of empty bottles of a patent medicine, Dr. Krohn's Gold Cure. Someone moaned outside the nearest cabin. The figure was lying on a grey blanket, her skin bubbling in the sun. The younger children seemed not to be affected by the plague. They ran around the outskirts of the little settlement. Their innocent games seemed a world away from the scenes of sickness and suffering inside the cabins. But there was no knowing how many of them had already died.

One of the photographs showed a man dressed in the ragged remains of a morning suit. The shirt had long ago fallen apart, but he still wore the pathetic bowtie around his dirty throat. It was a frightening face. His forehead bulged like a ball, and he had long matted hair and oriental eyes. It was such a startling face that Turner asked the photographer about him.

"There is more than one strange hermit living in the woods," Van Schaick replied. Then he went on, "Our experiments have reached a particularly interesting stage. They are producing some very remarkable results." Van Schaick offered Turner another set of prints to examine.

Turner realized that he was looking at an example of their spirit photography. For some reason, there were large white shadows on these prints, as though the method of printing had been flawed. This "darkness in the glass" was quite mystifying, Van Schaick told him. It was something he had never come across before in his professional experience. Dark stains had appeared in the emulsion on the glass plates, and became these suggestive white shapes in the positive prints. "Look," he said. "I'll show you what I mean."

The emulsion had begun to go powdery on some of the glass plates, and there were dark stains, as though sepia had been spilt. There was something else, Van Schaick said.

During their attempts to photograph spectral presences that summer, a mysterious figure had appeared on the other side of the lake, a young Indian woman who left no tracks and no history, but whose ghostly speech continued to reverberate in Temple Woods.

As Turner lifted the next photograph from the stack, the lost face appeared before him. There was a shimmering effect, like the afternoon sunlight on the lake. The hair was drawn back from her face and the light coming from behind her like that made her head seem bigger. For a fleeting moment, the face seemed to compose itself anew, before her features began to dissolve, and the face of Jane Whitecloud for a second time disappeared.

Turner felt he was actually there at the lake shore, in the misty trees of Temple Woods, an observer of everything that had passed within these chronicles of glass. Her eyes looked back at him with the same shyness and uncertainty as they always had. In each subsequent print, her features were more difficult to make out. The light of childhood, which had been plain innocent daylight by the lake, had somehow been spent. A kind of darkness had begun to suffuse those photographs. Her face had been eaten away. The glacier of history had stolen down and obliterated her.

Now Turner finally came out with the question he only now realized had been behind his coming to the photographer's in the first place. "But what is Madame L'Allemand's purpose in all these experiments? What precisely is she trying to achieve?"

There was surprise in the photographer's response. "Come now. Don't you know? Pauline is a medium. One of the best I've ever seen. She talks to those poor spirits in the woods. Talks to the lost girls. Those girls who disappeared in the woods."

While singing, Pauline L'Allemand often had the sensation of being joined by other voices, a spectral choir from "the other side." These "visitors" were like real presences in the room, as physical as marble statues, which seemed to exude coolness. She spent hours with the books of Madame Blavatsky, and her automatic writing. She was a regular correspondent with Colonel Olcott of the Theosophical Society in New York in her attempts to discover the whereabouts of the lost girls.

She had seen many grieving spirits in the forest that summer, but the one she could not forget was the naked girl with skin the color of tobacco, rising up before them like smoke from the trees, leading them further into Temple Woods. Pauline felt close to this grieving spirit whose cries continued to echo in the woods, but she couldn't understand exactly what she was saying.

Pauline L'Allemand had trained at the conservatorium in Dresden and made her debut in Königsberg. She had performed in the great opera houses of Europe and dined with kings. No one in her audience would have suspected that, back at her lodgings, cared for by a maidservant, there was a child. She still kept the old programs of the operas in which she had appeared, her messages of congratulations and old photographs tied into bundles with pink ribbons.

While she was studying in Europe, Pauline sometimes used to speak of a man, a terrifying figure from her past, whom she called "The Necromancer." These trances of hers were like a storm, everything was dark, and Pauline was afraid. She had even undergone a course of hypnosis in an effort to rid herself of these terrifying visitations. Then one night she got suddenly worse. To Pauline it seemed that there was something waiting for her, some evil force which saw its chance and leapt. They found her on the floor of her dressing room, flailing her arms, lashing out at phantoms. There was real suffering in her face, and those who found her did not doubt that she really was in the grip of some spirit power.

Years before, when she had been plain Pauline Elhasser, she had begun singing in a traveling circus. In her circus photograph she is about sixteen, wearing a dress of sequins, revealing her bare arms, and a flounced taffeta skirt. On her feet she wears the soft slippers of a dancer or a tightrope walker. She is sitting on an orange crate beside a man who bears a resemblance to Edgar. There is the same thick, wavy hair, the straight nose, the dreamer's eyes. And yet there is something of the wolf about this man. There is a faint snarl on his lips, the beginning of a sarcastic smile. Those bored eyes of his have a look of sleepy cunning. There is something about his face which could be Russian.

Though she had claimed to be American born, her slight German accent gave to her speech a hint of regret, even bitterness. There was something about the way she held her mouth that suggested she was a little hurt to find herself here in Wisconsin, in this lost place at the edge of the great forest.

Had there really ever been a Count L'Allemand? Somehow Turner doubted it. She did not wear a wedding ring out of devotion to the memory of a husband. And who was this mysterious father of Edgar's who had seduced her in the circus, a man who had brought so much shame on her that she could not even now bear to mention his name?

She had loved the circus, the color, the noise, the smell of sweat and animal dung and food all mixed together. He had worked upon her heart by enchantment. He showed disdain toward Pauline, as if he had judged her character and found it wanting. And so she thought: "If I go crawling to him . . . Perhaps if I can offer something to him, anything he wants, even my soul!"

His voice had a soporific effect on her and she couldn't stay awake. The feeling of heaviness spread through her limbs and she fell into a dreamless sleep. Next thing she knew she was going to have Edgar.

Edgar had wanted to be an acrobat, to perform in the circus; then he had contracted poliomyelitis. As soon as Edgar found himself stuck with a brace on his leg, Pauline made up her mind to wipe all his youthful aspirations out of his memory, just exactly as though they had never existed. It was intolerable for her to think that those happy thoughts should torment him.

To help finance the production of *De Capite de Confusis*, the opera she had written, Pauline had sold everything. She had borrowed money, too, on the confident prediction of the opera's assured success. After the fiasco in Milwaukee, when she had to flee her creditors and start a new life, she had been reduced to working "upstairs" in the Shanghai House Hotel in Black River Falls.

At first, the ladies of Black River Falls had been keen to make Pauline's acquaintance. There was even a little competition to become her first intimate friend, this famous opera singer with her airs and graces, her exaggerated bustle under her Parisian silk. Then word had got around that she had taken lodgings "upstairs" at the Shanghai House. People looked at her in a different way. Women in the street would cover their mouths and begin to whisper as soon as she had passed.

After two weeks at Heartsease she had the feeling there was someone hiding in the trees, watching her. She told Edgar and he said he could sense it too, to stay indoors and away from the windows. Pauline was convinced that the authorities in Milwaukee had sent a man to find them, in connection with their unpaid bills from *De Capite de Confusis*. There was a Pinkerton's man who had been asking questions about them in Milwaukee, before they had fled.

There were other puzzling events, too. Pauline believed in the power of the ancient spirits of this land, but she could not understand why the hen had been nailed to the barn door. Then one day Van Schaick had photographed a strange hermit in the woods with a clay face and a ragged morning suit. Pauline had immediately recognized him.

Pauline L'Allemand had tried to break away from the power this man from her past held over her, but there was no use. It was a life sentence. Sometimes she believed she might have broken his spell; but even now, after the passage of so much time, when her career was gone, all her hopes in life reduced to puny dimensions, even after all these years, there were moments when she heard him talking again. Not the particular words, just the quiet sound of his voice was enough to bring her screaming awake in the bed, her hair stuck to her face, wet with perspiration.

Several days of rain kept Turner indoors. From his attic window at the inn he looked out over the slippery shingles to the misty pine forest. Without success he attempted to compose some notes for his paper on the frontier. He spent two of those days in his bed, under the mosquito net, shivering with fever, with his whiskey bottle and tumbler.

When he left his room and went downstairs again, he saw Edgar in the drinking lounge. The regulars were used to seeing the well-dressed young man who carried around his telescope and played his aluminum violin for nickels and pennies to pay for his drinks. Turner had seen him on the Wazee trail with that baby shotgun of his, the little 20-gauge with the hexagonal barrel. But now Edgar stared past Turner. His Adam's apple worked up and down in his throat against his collar stud, and his attention was preoccupied with something else.

Edgar stood there, his handsome head slightly to one side, his thumbs hooked in the pockets of his blue silk waistcoat. Edgar had just reached the age when he was interested in girls. There was one girl in particular he liked, a small-framed blonde girl with unusually pale skin. She only had to look in his direction for Edgar to be at her side, charming, smiling. He had inherited his mother's love of attention. The girl seemed annoyed by Edgar, though, and avoided the young man with his leg brace and his aluminum violin.

The three of them made their way through Temple Woods to the place where the wind creaked in the hemlock trees. At one point, Turner stopped to pick some golden chanterelle mushrooms. He considered himself an expert in the botany of the summer woods, but he had never before seen them growing in pine needles, which were too acidic to support anything much.

Van Schaick carried his camera over his shoulder, holding it by its folding wooden legs. Pauline was dressed like some minister's wife, with her navy blue skirt and jacket; quite a contrast to the garish stage clothes she usually wore. Edgar had not accompanied them. They made their way through the trees. Their feet were soundless on the forest floor, as though no sound could survive in the presence of this greater silence. When they spoke to each other—a single word, "Here?," answered by another word, "Further"—their voices were puny, diminished.

They passed an Ojibwa burial ground: miniature bark lodges, coffins above the ground with pitched roofs. They came at last to the patch of blackened ground. There were white bones in the ashes. It was here they burned the bodies and belongings of the Indians who had died from diphtheria. Pauline's face showed no fear or shock at the sight of this obscene ossuary, and Turner instantly understood why. She had come to this ritual place of death before.

Pauline began to unpack her rucksack. From where

Turner stood, its contents looked like bundles of clothes. She took a white shawl and placed it over her head, as if this gesture were demanded by decency, or as if she were entering a church. She began to pray aloud, "Great Father, give these poor bones your blessing, grant to these unquiet souls the peace of the Great Universal Spirit . . ."

Pauline began to sing. She opened her mouth and that pure sound poured out, but it was not like her usual performance. This was not the merriment of a polite evening's entertainment, but something darker. Pauline's voice answered something in Turner himself which he could not identify, exactly. Her song was poisoning the air.

She held the note, dark and sweet, for a long time. Even when it seemed she must surely now break off and draw breath she held the note, her dark eyes gazing at the same spot in the trees on the other side of the clearing, and Turner marveled at that voice which seemed big enough to contain another world, the world she always sang about, the world of the gods, the world of thunder. Turner wanted to jump to his feet and intervene, tell her to put a stop to this voice which contained another world.

Still she maintained that single note, her expression one of triumph, and it occurred to Turner that she might be seeing not these trees at the edge of a vast forest in the New World, but the audience which had included a king in her debut performance in Königsberg. The sound of the wind in the pine trees seemed to form itself into a woman sighing, moaning: coming out of the dream and back into the world. When Pauline looked up, Turner saw the look of fear and wonder on her face. She stood there for a long time without moving. Something had changed in her. She seemed unwell. He saw the white tension in her nostrils. Everything about her seemed wrong. She suffered. She was confused. The trance had never come upon her this way before. She spoke words that made no sense. Something was rotting on the forest floor!

Pauline let out a cry, and covered her mouth and nose with her hand. But she continued to see that face, the suffering contorted mask her own face had become. Turner heard the whispering sound of the wind approaching. "The strychnine," Pauline said. She spoke in a voice that was not her own. "To help me out of my misery."

Turner realized that in the trees on the other side of the clearing was a solitary figure. There were leaves and grass caught up in her owl-feather cloak, and more feathers and grass in her long matted black hair. Her skin was covered in feces and grass. She looked like she had been buried. He stood very still and stared at the spirit girl, at the aura of outrage which shrouded the clearing in the woods. Sunlight leaked in through the foliage of the trees. He stared at her, trying to fix her in his mind, memorizing every detail of her, before she should vanish again.

She was holding something in her hand, which might have been a small bottle. She held up the bottle. She drank. Her mouth twisted up, as if she had just tasted something exceptionally bitter. Some minutes passed. The muscles of her body began to twitch and she seemed to have difficulty breathing. Then suddenly her whole body arched and her head bent violently backward, her mouth fell open and her eyes strained back in her head, looking up to the heavens. A minute later, her body relaxed and she fell back on the ground. The flower of forgetfulness bloomed through her flesh and she was gone. The bile-colored light leaked through the trees where she had been.

"Well, now she's gone and there's nothing you can do to bring her back," Pauline said. The noise she made was like someone struggling for breath, the sound of someone suffocating.

5

BILLY SUNDAY

It was unusually quiet in Temple Woods that day, a sense of hushed expectation, as though something demanded such silence. It had been here that the old Indian temples had been found, the mounds of painted rocks. Some of the places were still used by local bands of Winnebagos and Ojibwa for their ceremonies. An unsuspecting hunter would sometimes come across Manitou objects, plates and bottles hanging from a particular tree, or feel the drips of fresh blood and look up to see a newly sacrificed cockerel hanging from the branch overhead.

The air was warm, heavy, humid at this time of year. There was the sluggish drone of honeybees, a spicy cinnamon fragrance to the sunshine. Here, blocks of sunlight lay upon the glade, broken up by long bars of shadow from the tall trees. The droning sound grew more intense. First one then another insect landed on his face. They proved not to be honeybees, but big glossy green-black flies. The further into the glade Billy Sunday's footsteps took him, the more flies there were. It was as though the air were alive with them.

He saw that at the far side of the glade some trees had been felled. He realized that he was on the edge of an old slashing, though the second growth was already well established. Corridors of trees had been felled to let the hauling teams in, and these now made pathways of light, lit up the forest floor in that otherwise dark damp place, and the mellow light played over the shapes and contours of the soft mossy ground. There were mounds and hillocks, shallow pits, and now he recognized the pile of rotten logs which had been left there, either because they had been rotten then and rejected, or because they had just been forgotten, covered with poison oak and ivy. The ivy was like a carpet thick upon the ground, which climbed up the trunks of the trees.

He heard the chuck-chuck of an axe, a common sound in the woods, the rasping of a saw, the hollow scattergun of a woodpecker. There came the sound of a falling branch from somewhere, the slow creaking of separation, the eternity of waiting or falling; then the crashing to earth, which seemed to live on for a full minute as a kind of supernatural applause.

Billy Sunday came out at the slashing where loggers had been. There was a track leading out of the other side of the slashing, with wheel ruts from the wagons. The narrow track led up the grassy hill.

He kept thinking about the stains on the glass plates, their shadowy lines fluid, changing. The further Billy Sunday went, the further he invaded sacred ground, the domain of those Indians whose silent staring presence, part stony witness, part rebuke, had begun to fill him with such dread. At one stage, traveling back toward the Wazee, he thought he could hear the river close by, water rushing over rocks.

Billy Sunday felt sharp points of light flecking across his back, inducing the illusion of coldness. He felt himself under the goad, and saw those creatures who could only be part of Indian magic join him in his woodlands imagination. Temple Woods seemed a world that existed before he was awake, and now by some miracle, he had wakened into it: a world inspired by a single breath of pure wonder. And in that moment, Billy Sunday felt his heart galloping in his chest, his breath held tight, and he knew he had been granted access to the mystic landscape which he entered at night through the trees into the relief of dreamless sleep, into the world of white, the tundra of not-being.

The wind in the trees was like a voice which moved in and whispered to him, flowed through him, a voice which rose in dream above the trees. The woods closed around him. And all the time the voice led him deeper into the dreaming trees.

The bright air seemed to be bursting with silent elation. A shrill keening sound filled his ears, and he knew he was hearing the voice of Pauline L'Allemand again, trapped there, from that first day in the forest. High up, lit by the sun, the trunks of trees were like the texture of stone, a world of light above the darkness of the forest. Pauline's voice was in the sound of water. The trees breathed her, and she was there in the shadow of a girl who had once moved along the forest floor among the bright lichens and ferns, dark ivy.

Then, just ahead, there was something which made him stop.

It was something dead on the forest floor, the bloated carcass of an animal that had begun to rot and sink into the matted vegetation. It looked soft and damp, the same dark color as the forest floor. The limbs were the contorted shapes of the roots of trees. They looked as though they had been arrested in movement, writhing in the air.

When his toe touched it, he was suddenly lost in wonderment, a soft privateness, a cocoon of not-seeing which separated him from the thing. It was a piece of human flesh, not big: the back of a hand which had gone grey, the same color as the scum which congeals around the top of the copper when soap is being made. Only recently had the black patches of putrefaction begun to spread. This hand, which seemed to grasp out of the earth, might have belonged to someone lost under heavy snow.

As he stared at it his eyes began to adjust to the sight, the changed dimensions of the world. It was like a big lump of lichen which had survived all that winter under the dark weight of the snow. In that long age of ice, the floor of the woods had disappeared altogether, and he thought now of this slow miracle after the snow had melted, and the damp summer had laid bare to the world again the secret in the dark heart of the dream, the old shape pushing up into the fresh world, corrupting the spicy smell of the cedars in the air.

He could see the shape of every rib, the sunken orb of the cranium, the kneecaps protruding through the mulch of leaves. He was held by the horror of it; he could not move away. The smell of her was everywhere, in the air, in the water; in the sound of the swarming flies. The streaks of stain where she had begun to rot and the flesh collapsed looked as though she had been shaped by soiled hands. As he stared, he became that little world of the body. He joined the ants in brain and eye and hand, charging into the object and in this way was joined to its fate.

He let out a loud cry, as though he were in pain, then quickly clamped his hand to his face, squeezing together the nostrils and covering his mouth. His eyes were watering from the stench coming up from the earth. He hated it, but he couldn't take his eyes away from it. Another understanding of the world had pushed up into his life, and it compelled him, commanded him.

After the shock and revulsion, then the intense interest, now there was a feeling of tremendous excitement. He felt the wild elation ripping through his body. From that sight of decay and corruption, blank staring death, now there came a wave of almost unbearable energy.

He was running, but now the contours of the land followed the shapes of death on the forest floor. It was strange he didn't fall, he was running so fast, scrambling over roots of trees like ribs, ridge and curve of bone, great swelling bole of cranium. It was like traveling through a graveyard in a dream. He was still back there, really, filling himself with the sight, heavy with the horror. He was still being taken into the body, his own weight sinking down into the dark wet earth.

The landscape he traveled through was tired and grey, swampy and overgrown with goldenrod. He made his way through these fields of water, past these trees with no branches. He was running through a dead landscape of mud and stench, a battlefield. As he ran, the bare tree trunks were great black poles of shadow pulsing across the screen of his eyes.

He wondered if he had died back there, and this region he was passing through was a kind of hell. His running feet moved effortlessly, as if of their own accord, as if it were they alone and not all his shrieking self who was intent on fleeing that place, fleeing that person in whose unwholesome grey flesh the gaze continued to sink as though there were no rock bottom to the seeing.

The passing trees began to pulse across his vision more and more rapidly. He heard a violent turbulence somewhere, and realized he must be near Manitou Falls, its thunder carrying through the forest. Then the pulses beating across the screen came at intervals further apart, became cool caves of retreat from the halo of sun burning down on his head.

There was a croaking noise in his ears all the time, like the slow splintering sound of a tree falling. The Indian bark-peelers stopped work and watched him pass. He kept running, following the contours of death on the forest floor, looking straight ahead, not daring to stop or to look back at them.

6

FREDERICK JACKSON TURNER

He was back in Temple Woods again.

Turner lay back against the trunk of the cedar and lit his pipe, losing himself in the tobacco trance. There was a sultry stillness about the woods in the afternoons which affected him in a peculiar way.

The trees were dreaming in glass on the surface of the lake; the lake shore was as still as sleep. In the middle of the lake was a group of small floating islands, vegetation sprouting from mats of sedge, each like an afterthought of the forest, the last few drops shaken from the dream. All was stillness. A fly buzzed. Lake trout began to rise and feed. The birch-bark canoe hovered there on the lake, suspended from time, seeming never to get closer. He concentrated on the surface of the lake, willing her to reappear.

At last, faint circles formed in the silky surface of the water. The spell was broken, the phantom trees wobbled in the glass and vanished, and the circles spread steadily wider until one after another they lapped against the shore. He continued to gaze toward the dark line of trees on the other side, until the copper light shining off the water lit up his face, filled it with a look of almost unbearable expectation.

A feeling of excitement flowed through him, which was almost sexual in its intensity. For nearly an hour he lay there, gazing out across the lake, hardly daring to move his head. Then he heard the dip of the paddle, and saw the rings spread out across the surface of the water, lapping against the shore.

It was an old birch-bark canoe, half sunken in the water, smelling of fish. She must have come to bathe in the lake, and by chance beached the canoe at just this point. And yet the solitary figure came nearer, approaching him as though she had some claim upon him. He thought that soon the chimera would evaporate and he would be left with the romantic vista of the lake again. Now quite definitely, Jane Whitecloud turned to him with carnal intention in her eyes.

Turner had the feeling just then that those eyes had seen him every moment of his life. There was nothing he could hide from her. She had seen everything he had ever done and thought and felt. She saw and knew and understood— he had been about to use the word "forgave."

She was here again, seeking the poetry, safely hidden away within the walls of the trees, transfigured by the secrets of the forest. Although the daydreaming of it was innocent enough, its extreme vividness was cause for concern: there was no way of knowing where such an intoxication of the spirit might end. How had he lost himself in these woods, alone with a silent Indian girl—a girl who seemed intent on keeping her silence? What he felt was the stirring of desire; and what man did not have such secrets in his heart? He was a member of a vast and secret brotherhood.

She took him into her where it was warm, where the sun had been. All the time he was lost in her warm moaning, in that space of sunlight and water, he heard the other sound, steady, rhythmic, the chugging of the steamer in the afternoon, on its way to the Indian mission.

He knew every contour of her body, every inch of her tawny young skin; the luster of her black hair, the mossy mound of her pelt. As they made love on the forest floor, they became muddy. She was the body of the soil itself. Her slim body, dark as wood, with her long breasts, had the fish smell of the shallow brown lake, the faint odor of rotting salmon on the rocks of the dry riverbed in winter. She was soil shaped by the worship of human hands. He bit into the soft part of her upper arm, and later he would be able to make out the shape of his teeth still there, next to the lines of her tattoo.

Now it swept over him as always with such speed and rage he felt himself drowning. She knelt and pointed her spine straight at his heart. He disappeared inside her. She let out a scream: he had filled her with hot pain. He butted into her hard. The distressed sound she made excited him, a feeling from another time, and at that moment Turner knew he recognized that look on the girl's face, not just shock or disapproval, but a look of outrage and pain. Her eyes were suddenly full of light, showing the same fear she had on the first afternoon. Her breath heaved from her chest, smelling of sour herbs. The dazzling sunlight off the lake seemed harsh, too heartless a light for a lover to appear in.

Afterward they lay in the little lakeside clearing, with its mulch of black leaves, the smell of feces in the air. The Indian girl offered him no answer to his questions. Her arms were wings, wrapped in her cloak of shivering owl feathers. She looked as though she was made of tiny birds, as though her body was alive with birds, shivering with tiny life. He loved her slim neck, her tattoo, her thick black hair. He wanted to stay with her all night here in the woods. He closed his eyes and brought her dear head close to his, so that the skin of their faces was touching. Seeing the tender skin of her young belly made him shudder. Turner felt the earthworms crawling down through his viscera, the sour taste of his vomit rising into his mouth.

It seemed strange that he should hear a piano just then, the sound of a piano so deep in the woods, miles from the nearest civilization. The piano notes carried as clearly as though he had been standing outside someone's parlor. The music gradually faded away, lost somewhere in the cathedral of the trees.

Turner lay there, waiting to hear the sound of Pauline singing again; but instead he heard the distant chugging of the wood-burning steamer, the scraps of human voices flung in the wind, the faint murmurs and moans from the Indian mission along the shore of the lake. The breeze across the surface of the lake carried sounds of trumpeting elephants, circus animals, a sound like a girl screaming.

At last the sound of the screams from across the lake faded. The woods settled into a frightened silence. He was awake. He lay very still under the cedar tree. He felt cold. He heard the rustle of branches moving in the breeze. He lay there and watched the icy stars appear in the evening sky.

He willed her to come back. But she did not come back.

7

BILLY SUNDAY

Billy Sunday running along the trail, his face white with terror. The fisherman, a solitary figure in his old felt hat, waders and tackle vest, dark patches at the armpits of his shirt. Turner, the man alone, knees drawn up, back against the dreaming tree, not fishing, just staring.

Turner heard the sound of someone coming through the trees. He looked up in surprise at this sudden intrusion into his private world. The boy seemed not to notice Turner. He still believed himself to be quite alone on this ancestral trail through the woods. Turner wondered what had brought the young laborer into this gloomy, haunted realm. He was wearing his undershirt, and his trousers were dirty from work.

Then their eyes met and Billy Sunday let out an exclamation. The boy was frightened. The breath came noisy out of his nostrils. Billy Sunday's eyes, like his name, were full of light. Billy Sunday looked back at the man with his rubber trousers, hating him. In panic he turned and began to run back in the direction he had come from, toward the slashing. Turner called to him, "Hold on, there."

Billy Sunday did not answer.

"Are you deaf?" Turner called after him. "You look absolutely amazed about something." But Billy Sunday had already run on along the trail.

Billy Sunday made his way to the dark porch with the ox-yoke lintel. He was trembling, trying to speak. He had a look of intense effort on his face, and he was making an incoherent noise, his tongue tugging at the roots of something which existed only in his brain.

"A dead girl? Here?" Edgar was incredulous. Creases remained in his cheeks after he had stopped smiling, after he saw it was not a joke. Edgar reached for his whiskey bottle and took a long drink. Since his arrival at Heartsease, Edgar had often teased Billy Sunday. There was a streak of cruelty in the crippled boy with his telescope and aluminum violin.

Perspiration ran down Billy Sunday's face. There was a bad smell, like foul pondage, and the legs of his trousers were wet. Billy Sunday felt unsteady on his feet. His legs felt like they were not connected with his body. He suddenly began to retch. He staggered into the dark kitchen, to the tin washstand. The thin vomit floated on the cold water.

Billy Sunday did not say anything else for a long time. He sat, trembling, mute with terror, staring into space. Then, he told Edgar about what he had found in the trees, its shape and smell.

"Jesus, Billy Sunday," said Edgar. "Why did you ever have to go and find her?"

Then everything went very quiet.

"Oh, hell, don't you see? It's Twyla Flake. They'll think you did it. They'll come after you. They'll bring Indian trackers with them. They'll bring Tom Thunder. You can swear on that damn Bible of yours all you like. They'll say you're lying. They'll say you did it. And who's to say you didn't? Who's to tell them what's the truth about what happened? Oh, they'll think you did it, all right."

"You're a liar. You're drunk and you're a liar." Billy Sunday's eyes were straining in his head, like a frightened horse.

"It's all right to be scared," Edgar said. "You just be as scared as you damn well like."

"I'll kill you," Billy Sunday said, but his voice was flat, without conviction.

"You won't kill anyone else."

"Don't think I never killed a man. Once I killed a man near Oshkosh. He was a tramp and I had to do it."

"Then tell me how you did it. Did you use a knife?"

"I did it with a tent peg," Billy Sunday said. "I made a hole in the back of his head so big his brains came out."

"You did no such thing."

"I did it all right."

"Oh, hell, Billy Sunday," he said. "Why did you ever have to go and find her?"

Billy Sunday went back with Edgar and the Rhinelander brothers, Moses and Jacob. He led them down to that strange piece of earth he had found growing under the tree.

The Rhinelanders began digging with their spades underneath the tree, in the hollow of the great bulging roots. They knelt, with their spades underneath that human shape, but when they tried to lift it, the shape collapsed back into the earth. When they stood up, their overalls were caked with mud at the knees. There was no girl here. It was just tree.

None of them believed that Billy Sunday had just imagined it. Edgar said he must have found the girl, all right, but he had brought them to the wrong place in order to conceal his crime.

Jacob Rhinelander said he had a mind to shoot the boy right there, and that they would fetch the dogs again from Griffith's farm to sniff her out. Then Moses said he had a better idea.

Billy Sunday sat on the lakeshore. There were other men now, as well as the Rhinelanders and Edgar. His shirt had been torn from his back, and he was barefoot. He had been leg-roped, and his hands tied. The legs of his trousers were stained. They encouraged him to tell them what he knew about Twyla Flake. He sat there motionless for several minutes, then began to move his head in a peculiar manner, moving his mouth, though no words came out. Fear pulled his face tight, and his mouth twitched.

Billy Sunday had just seen that a thick rope had been secured on the overhanging branch. The roaring of the blood in his head was so intense, for a few moments he could not hear what they were saying. His clothes felt unbearably tight. When the roaring of his blood subsided, it left him feeling weak. He could hardly stand, and he was shivering like a frightened animal.

"I think the boy wants some convincing," Jacob Rhinelander said. Perspiration glistened on his forehead, and there were damp patches on his shirt.

Moses Rhinelander said, "If I am any judge of boys, the noose will have no trouble convincing him."

"I don't know where she is," Billy Sunday said.

"Then know about the rope."

Billy Sunday could not have known it was just a ruse to get him to confess to his crime. As he saw the tree he felt a sensation spreading up through his stomach in cold points of panic. He made himself look at the branch with the rope swinging gently back and forth, a movement too gentle for such a monstrous sight.

Jacob signaled the other men, and Billy Sunday was brought forward under the branch. They dragged him, and his tied feet made a furrow in the soft pine needles.

Now that the moment was near, all of them were afraid. Billy Sunday could see in their faces, all the men, even those who had been loudest and meanest before. And he knew that their fear was good reason for him to have fear, too.

The boy would talk, they said. He had to talk now. But it

was the way Billy Sunday just looked back at them that infuriated them. They seemed intent on hanging him now, and yelled all kinds of insults as they prepared the noose. In a fury of movement, the noose was around Billy Sunday's neck, two of the men were pulling on the other end, making it support all of his weight, and Billy Sunday's feet had left the ground. He made an excited sound, trying to get air.

From somewhere behind him, Billy Sunday heard the loose sound of dirt and stones sliding from the pan of the spade. Billy Sunday knew they were digging a grave for him. Now they put the rope around his neck again and strung him up. All at once he felt the pressure of the rope and his feet left the ground.

He was overcome by the sensation of strangulation, but one of the men supported his body just enough that he did not pass out. They set him down a second time and as soon as he was able to breathe again, they asked him once more what he knew about the girl. Billy Sunday began to speak again, but still no words came out. He saw his life pass before his eyes, at the rancid lakeside clearing. He saw himself on his own deathbed, in a prison hospital, it looked like; and he felt terror when he saw what kind of future lay ahead of him. It just did not seem possible that he would end his days like that. He could not escape the seeing.

A new figure approached, walking around the lake shore toward the little clearing. It was Robertson, a man Billy Sunday had seen often at the inn at Balsam Point. He said he was from the Chicago office of Pinkerton's Detective Agency. He had been hired by the Flake family to find out what had happened to their daughter. "You have heard about the girl, Twyla Flake, who disappeared last week?" He looked at Billy Sunday. "They are serious. Deadly serious," he said.

Billy Sunday said, "I beg you, Mister. Just tell them to stop. I didn't kill her. I don't even know who she is. I found her in the trees and then when we went back she was gone and that's all I know and that's the honest truth, honest to God."

Jacob Rhinelander, who that year had put two of his own small children in the churchyard from diphtheria next to all the other wooden crosses, said, "Why should we believe the word of a half-caste?"

"We ought to just shoot him and get it over with," said Edgar aggressively. He knew the local people laughed at him as a cripple, as well as at his attire, his blue silk waistcoat and his beautiful long black eyelashes that would have been more fitting on a daughter. He stood with his little 20-gauge with its hexagonal barrel, but made no move to use it.

They yanked Billy Sunday up for a third time. His body began to swing back and forth very slowly in the afternoon breeze. He was still breathing when they finally let him down, but he had passed out. They lay him on the freshly dug ground. They would take him by boat to Sheriff Buckley and let *him* get to the truth.

At the end of the dock, the wood-burning steamer, *The Lady of the Lake*, rocked gently in the water. When the boat bumped against the dock Billy Sunday felt the pylons move under his feet. The afternoon sun cast a strong bronze light over the surface of the water. An unnatural calm had descended on the lake. His captors had untied his hands, but they still stood around him, guarding him. Some of the men from the inn wandered along the dock with their drinks to look at him.

An hour later Billy Sunday was still standing in the same place, looking toward the far shore, where the line of black trees stretched north into Canada, to the ice, to the hard, final line at the top of the world. The deckhand, who had been checking the lines, came across to the other side of the boat to see what was the matter when he saw the boy jump from the dock. They emptied all the cartridges in their rifles into the lake, spotting the surface like rain.

Billy Sunday knew he was drowning. He could feel the tight pressure in his lungs, the pain in his ears and, even as he was sinking, the ringing of the greater silence to come. He passed through layers of darkness and light. Above the surface of the water, the sky was humid pearl. The surface of the water was choppy, as though there was going to be a storm, and the boat continued to bump gently against the side of the dock. He saw, as he sank deeper, the bottom of the boat, *The Lady of the Lake*, with its bright patches of fouling, like russet algae.

The sudden bump as he hit the bottom of the lake surprised him. The object was blubbery, the skin shiny with oily rainbows, but it was the face in the water that terrified him. Billy Sunday looked at the hair trailing out above her in the water. He saw her arms rise on the current as her belt kept her anchored there, feet sunken in the mud. Now he could really see her, lit up in a band of light. As she moved slightly in the rhythm of the water, her hair fanned out and closed like an anemone. Her belt had been fastened around something, like an iron wheel and short axle, as one might find in a railroad yard. Then he saw it was the cider press from Heartsease.

He felt the wall of water pressing in upon his ears, upon the metallic-tasting membrane at the back of his nose and top of his throat. But the longer he remained on the floor of the lake, the more another order of reality which belonged to the surface world began to press in on him and to transform him. The longer he spent at the bottom of the water, the more he felt himself rising, breaking the skin of the lake's surface, bursting into air, and, miraculously, continuing to rise into space. He rose up through the intense stream of light. Bullets from the men on the shore blistered the surface of the lake.

He had no idea how that act of rising had taken place, but in the moment of his release through the skin of the water, Billy Sunday became again the innocent boy who had gone fishing last summer, before he had even seen the photographer, before Pauline and her clairvoyance and spirit photography, a time when the world was still as simple as looking forward to the day when three barrels of apples and a rusty cider press would be his.

As Billy Sunday swam toward the far shore, the shooting stopped, and the water through which he moved now seemed unnaturally calm. The last man to fire unshouldered his rifle, not wanting to waste any more ammunition. The boy could not possibly have survived all that.

When Billy Sunday finally scrambled up the muddy bank, he was startled to find that he was completely naked. His captors had stripped him to his pants to hang him, but these had come away off him in the water, and now as he disappeared into the mud and trees on the other side of the lake he was a primordial creature.

He did not think, but simply ran, and he did not stop running until he was far away. He felt he was running past the world, past all the faces he had ever seen, the faces in the timber camps and in the churches, the faces in the freak shows, gnarled and contorted. The life he had seen had been a phantasmagoria of suffering. Yet now, as he ran for his life, he felt that something had changed. The world with its brightly painted figures was turning as calmly as a carousel. He ran past the wolves that had been watching him all evening from the line of the trees, their gaze absorbed in his flesh as though their teeth had already begun to enter it.

It was late in the night, an hour or two before dawn by the time he got to the railroad. He had crouched in the woods through a violent storm, and when the sky was lit up, he had seen it was but a little way to the bend in the Soo Line. As he approached cautiously through the line of trees, Billy Sunday heard the thump of the approaching locomotive. Then he could make out the shapes of the cars of the circus train, and hear the trumpeting of the elephants.

From there it was an easy thing, once the train had slowed for the bend, to reach out and pull himself up onto the step of the painted wagon and from there, wedge himself safely between cars while the train got up to speed again, and the door would open and he would find some clothes.

Billy Sunday was already moving around the edge of the lake, away from Balsam Point. The train's steam whistle sounded and to his amazement it was Pauline's voice, the way she had opened her mouth that first day and the pure keening sound had come out. He looked up and saw the figures carved in relief into the Columbia Band Wagon, golden-winged angels and cherubs, the ornate flowers and vines, the Stars and Stripes, and the beautifully carved face with her eyes frozen and mouth wide. It was the face he had seen at the bottom of the lake. All of this, Billy Sunday saw with the dubious clarity of a patient in fever.

8

FREDERICK JACKSON TURNER

Turner spent the evenings alone in his simple attic room at the inn at Balsam Point. He had grown accustomed to the narrow bed with its canopy of mosquito netting, the wicker chair, the unadorned, rough walls.

Billy Sunday's fate had frightened him. Suddenly, in the space of a single afternoon, everything had gotten out of control. He kept hearing a noise like someone struggling for breath, the sound of someone suffocating, and he thought of the drowning boy's face, sinking through the layers of light in the lake. Turner tried to concentrate on his reading, his maps. He told himself he was imagining things. He had an infection. He was feverish. These were tricks of the mind. But in the lonely nights, when his mind wandered, Billy Sunday was there again, like an intruder.

He awoke suddenly in the morning. Something had bumped, like the door being closed. He was awake, stiff with fright. He could make out a hazy figure on the other side of the mosquito net. Someone was sitting in the wicker chair beside the bed, watching him. But it was not the drowned face of the boy watching him; nor was it the familiar figure of the girl.

"Good morning!" Robertson said cheerfully. "Are you ill, Mister Turner? You look feverish all of a sudden."

Turner panicked. How did he get in here? I was especially careful to check that I had locked my door. He must have got the spare key from the clerk. What if he has already searched my room? Or perhaps he heard the noise in here last night and grew suspicious? Were Jane and I so noisy?

"Yes. I am very ill. Look here. What makes you think you can just come in here like this?"

"I can see that you are ill. I can observe that with my own eyes." Robertson looked the same as ever, the fat stomach straining against his shirt through the unbuttoned waistcoat, the red meaty face, the uncombed, tousled hair. He was Robert Robertson, Assistant Superintendent of Pinkerton's Detective Agency, in Chicago. He had been engaged by the family of Twyla Flake to inquire into the whereabouts of their daughter. Her family held grave fears that Twyla was the latest "disappearance."

"I don't mind telling you that it has been one of my favorite pastimes to observe my fellow creatures. I always say, if you can observe a human being, there's no cause to be bored, wherever you happen to find yourself."

"It seems that you have at least found the right profession."

"And I must say that I have learned more observing you than I have from watching most people."

"What is it you think you've learned?" But there was no real curiosity in Turner's question.

"I have learned my trade simply from observing my fellow man. You are somewhat withdrawn from people. Isn't that so? A bit of a loner?"

"Yes, this is quite true. I'm a keen fisherman. Fishermen tend to keep their own company."

"I am a great observer, as I said. And one of the things I have succeeded in observing about you is that you know a thing or two that I don't yet."

"I cannot begin to guess at what they might be."

"Yes, you are a keen fisherman. You've spent a great deal of time in Temple Woods, isn't that so?" Robertson paused, then added quickly, "You heard about what happened to Billy Sunday?"

Yes, Turner said. He had heard about it downstairs.

"Damned fool boy went and drowned himself rather than face the music, is what people say. But this is the thing that interests me. He said he saw a body in the woods. And when he went back—nothing. So we take the dogs in there. Still nothing. The whole thing just doesn't make sense. And I was wondering if *you* could help me find out about Twyla."

"What could you possibly mean?" Turner felt a tingling, numb sensation creep over his skin as though he were lowering himself into a too hot bath.

"This body he claimed he saw. I was hoping that we might have a little talk on that subject. That is, if you have no objection."

Robertson apologized for the inconvenience, especially since Turner was ill. "I do not wish to pry into your personal history. Merely to establish the activities of Billy Sunday during the time you were associated."

"There is nothing I can tell you. I saw him sometimes while I was fishing, that's all."

Robertson continued to look at Turner, with an expectant smile on his face, as if waiting for Turner to say something further. "Have you had much to do with these people, the photographer and his opera singer?"

Turner saw immediately that it was not being asked as a merely polite or trifling question. Turner felt the tide of unreasonable panic rise inside him. "I don't understand."

"What did you want with her?"

"What did I want? My purpose is to spend every day here fly-fishing."

"And yet, you made a visit to the Indian camp in their company. What—or who—did you expect to find in Temple Woods?"

Turner suddenly felt like shrieking with laughter.

"Who did you wish to contact? You see, I have had a conversation with our friend, the singer, on the subject. I've just come from their house. I would challenge anyone to make sense out of that little situation. The photographer claims that Billy Sunday is innocent of any wrongdoing. He objected in the strongest terms about the way the boy was treated. Van Schaick claims there is no body at all, but merely a 'spectral presence.' They even showed me some photographs—spirit photography, they called it—all foggy trees, it just looked like to me."

At the mention of Pauline, Turner burst out, "She makes those poor girls' disappearances into a parlor game. Well, I for one don't find it very amusing! Look. Whatever nonsense she might have told you has nothing to do with me. The lady is a chance acquaintance. How am I expected to understand such things? As an historian I am skeptical of the claims of spiritualists and Theosophists. I'm sorry I cannot be of more help to you."

"And yet you witnessed a rather remarkable performance," Robertson said. "I believe you were involved in an extraordinary communication."

"So. She 'sees' things. Or she claims to."

"And you. Did you *see* anything?"

"I saw her go into her contortions and the rest of it. All part of her craft she learned on the stage, I suppose. This clairvoyance of hers is in my opinion something of a charlatan's trick."

"And yet it might interest you to know that it is on the basis of her clairvoyance that she has made an accusation against Billy Sunday. Does that not disturb you? When Van Schaick left the room, Pauline told me confidentially that Billy Sunday had murdered all the girls, Twyla too. I have been able to confirm that he lived in the woods near here last summer, before he took up with that photographer. She claims she can 'see' a girl's body locked in a building. The loneliest place in the world, she says. She also claims another item of information from the Spirit World. She says that Billy Sunday is not dead."

"But how can that be? He perished in the lake, did he not?"

"As far as one can tell." Robertson had grown thoughtful again. "The afternoon the boy claimed to find the body of this—well, it might have been Twyla, for all we know. You saw him?"

"I was fishing. I saw the boy pass by on the trail. He seemed to be behaving strangely."

"How, exactly?"

"He looked frightened. Ill."

"Was there anything unusual you might have come across in the woods that afternoon?"

"If you mean the body of a girl then I must certainly disappoint you."

"Did you ever see Twyla Flake in the woods?" Robertson took from his waistcoat pocket a studio photograph of the girl.

"No. Do I understand you correctly? Are you making an accusation against me?"

Robertson did not answer at first. He sat back in the chair and made a ball shape with his hands, only the fingertips touching. He stared at the ceiling. When he finally spoke, it was as though Robertson was thinking aloud.

"Why should Turner here think I was accusing him of doing such a terrible thing? Does the simple fact that I'm inquiring about a missing girl—a girl who he had not even met, by his own admission—lead him to such a conclusion? If that's the case, then well, I am to blame. I ask your help in this matter as a professional man, a man of reason, as an historian, who might be used to weighing up evidence and reaching conclusions and all the rest of it. But I can see that

I've offended you and for that I am sincerely chastened."
Then Robertson added, "Your friend the singer tells me
that she saw a girl in the woods. A spirit she says. A spirit
no less! Well, we men of reason need not put too much cre-
dence in that. Except—maybe it was a real girl. And
except—you saw her too, so Pauline says."

"But I was delirious! They were hallucinations! My God,
man, I am sick, I told you. I have a fever, I can't think
straight. I'm pins and needles from head to toe, so please
don't torment me with any more of your questions." His
feeling of physical disgust had got the better of him, and he
was sure this was present in his face.

"Hallucinations, you say. You'll forgive me for thinking that you are beginning to sound like someone else
we know! Could it be that you are something of a
Theosophist, after all?" Robertson was suddenly irritable.
"You're not another follower of Madame Blavatsky, are
you? You're not another seeker of spiritual enlightenment
in the forest?"

"Really, Robertson. You are jumping to conclusions!"

"No, I'm not jumping to any conclusions," Robertson
said forcefully. He leaned forward in the wicker chair. "I
believe that you are a regular visitor up here. You turn up,
every July, regular as clockwork."

"As you know, I am a keen fisherman."

"You always ask for the same room. When you arrived
apparently there was some problem and you looked like
you were fit to cry. At least, so the clerk says. Anyway, I was
curious about how fine this room of yours is, seeing how it
is so special and everything, for you always to want to be
staying in it so badly. But now that I'm here, lo and behold,

it don't look so very special after all. Matter of fact, I'd say that my own room downstairs is superior." Robertson remained crouched forward in the chair, looking at him.

"Oh, it's easily explained. A sentimental attachment. I've been coming here to this inn for many years now, since childhood. I am something of a creature of habit. Yes, I can see that it might seem peculiar to some. This room holds fond memories for me. In connection with a lady friend. There is no mystery."

"Why, you are a romantic!" the detective exclaimed. "And are you not entitled to be? After all, it's not a crime, is it? To be a romantic? Why no. Not at all. I can understand a man with feelings. Notwithstanding my own rough and ready exterior, I am a feeling man myself. But to come back here year after year, insisting on staying in the same room, and not a very salubrious room at that, a dusty attic, I would describe it, looking around here now. A place fit for rats. Well, that kind of behavior seems to transcend a mere sentimental attachment."

"Don't say anything more!" Turner pleaded, raising his hand to his burning head.

Suddenly Robertson's manner changed. "What the hell do you keep coming back here for?" he demanded. "To prey on some other helpless girl, is it? To lure her into that stinking woods of yours? Last year a Memmie or a Sadie. This year a Twyla Flake? Well? Am I on the right track?"

"No!" Turner rose, anger darkening his face. The force of his denial brought him out of his bed. He felt like striking the man. He stood there in his nightgown, glaring down at the detective. Then, suddenly exhausted, he sat down again. "It is a sentimental affair. A personal matter, which concerns me alone. I had a friend who disappeared. A lady friend. Nothing to do with these cases you are talking about. It happened a long time ago. It goes without saying that this is a matter which requires the utmost discretion. I suppose that this will seem very shocking to you."

"I'm not as shocked as you think," said Robertson. "You have told me about an association in your past. A love affair. I don't know how I can remain delicate on this matter. What was the result of that association? How did it end?"

"To me it is still a mystery."

"And what is your solution to this mystery?"

"There is no solution. Just the same old questions and perplexities, and still she comes in the night, I don't know how many hundreds of times I have been woken by her voice, croaking and horrible. There are times in my life when I ask myself how I came to be so dreadfully unhappy." Turner lay back on the bed and pulled the mosquito net around him.

"Your ghost stories are entertaining, Turner. But if you think I have nothing better to do than to spend my hours trying to get to the bottom of some fathomless mystery— well, my job is to find the whereabouts of the Flake girl, dead or alive, no more, no less."

He rose to leave the attic room. "Actually, there was something else. I am a great observer, as I said. And I started to think to myself after that conversation we had that this Turner seems a pleasant chap, with his chatter about fishing and all the rest of it. Making conversation with me about the best trout streams. Always wearing his felt hat with his fishing flies stuck in the band. This fellow seems to be all too much of a fisherman. But then, why shouldn't he be pleasant, at the beginning of a month's vacation up here? Then, just three days later, he's wearing a very different expression. And guess what? He's packed and on the dock, impatient as can be. He looks more scared than a rabbit. So, I think to myself, something's changed for the worse for him. Now, what can it be? It can't be that the fishing is so very bad around here. The other sportsmen seem contented with their catches. I see racks of trout in the smokehouse. The ice shed is so full of fish there's hardly room for the milk pails, I believe. So whatever could it be that brought about such a big change in his plans? Could it just be that he's scared of the diphtheria? But now I find you've actually been to the Indian camp with this singer friend of yours. Why? I ask myself. There's not only the danger of infection from diphtheria. There are other pestilences there. Plague. Smallpox. It is a consequence of their lack of hygiene. Leprosy among the Indians is very bad."

Robertson paused, breathing noisily through his mouth. Turner could smell tobacco and methylated spirit on him. "So now I think to myself—what's his explanation? That he's seen a ghost? And I ask myself—would I expect anyone to believe me, if I came up with a story like that? Especially a history professor, who has to find a proper cause for everything. Nothing without a cause—isn't that what you fellows believe?"

That night Turner was awakened by the familiar touch on his shoulder. Jane crouched on the wicker chair in his room, a swaddle of bandages in her arms, like a baby, or a doll.

Her anguished expression seemed to accuse him of something. And when he saw that shivering cloak of owl feathers again, the cloak of the granddaughter of a Winnebago chief, he knew that there was something menacing about these visitations to his attic room. She looked different. There was something wrong with her. She just sat there at his bedside, mute. He caught a whiff of her cod liver oil smell. Sores had broken out around her cracked lips, where once he had kissed her and she had slipped her small tongue into his mouth. Now her tongue flicked out, touched the sores at the corner of her mouth, and tried to speak, but her voice did not rise above a hoarse croak.

"What is it you want from me?" he begged her.

"There's nowhere left to go," she said.

"What am I to do?"

But at that moment she vanished. Jane Whitecloud had fled the room, just as she had fled this world, and he was left without an answer to his question.

The next night she was back again. His sleep was broken by a sharp knock at the door. The jolt of being woken left him shaking. She was a noisy ghost. She knocked things over in his room. He was scared she would wake the other guests. He would wake later in the night with her warm tongue in his ear. In the early morning light he would open his eyes to see her standing in front of the big mirror.

Turner tried to think of a way he could quiet this nocturnal raider, so he would not have to listen to that croaking noise she made. But he had to accept her presence. He had no choice. He knew that this girl would continue to appear to him like this in her owl-feather cloak. Jane Whitecloud, or that part of her that remained in the world, would continue to intrude into his room at the inn at Balsam Point year after year, until her business with him was finished.

In the days following Billy Sunday's disappearance in the lake, the singer and the photographer kept to themselves. Only Edgar continued to come to the inn and sit all afternoon in the parlor, pestering the girls and playing tunes on his aluminum violin in return for rounds of whiskey.

Once they passed Turner on the logging road in the photographer's square black wagon. Turner removed his hat in greeting, waiting for them to stop. Van Schaick muttered "Good afternoon" with the barest civility, the singer looked away with a grave expression, ignoring him completely, and they drove on.

Turner could not understand her animosity toward him. He had done nothing to offend her, as far as he could see. But now she apparently held some grudge against him, whose cause he could not even begin to guess at. There was something else that worried him. She had apparently made an accusation against Billy Sunday. After their strange experience in the woods, she might make a similar, far-fetched accusation against Turner. She was, after all, a very unstable person. If he could have a confidential conversation with Pauline, she might agree to vouch for him. But the more Turner thought about what might be going on in Pauline's mind, the more he was frightened of her. Nevertheless, the next afternoon he forced himself to visit the house with the ox-yoke lintel hidden in the trees.

Turner was shocked by the injustice that had been done. He had tried to make himself believe Billy Sunday was guilty of the crimes, but his memory of the boy just did not sustain it. As far as he was concerned, Billy Sunday wanted nothing from the woods but the experience of a greater closeness to his Maker. He felt the pulse of God beat in his blood when he was in there. Billy Sunday had attended the Presbyterian church on Sunday mornings, dressed in clean clothes, that Indian hair of his slicked back with bear's grease. His expression was always meek and contrite. Billy Sunday had never gone anywhere without his Bible in his satchel. Turner remembered the night Billy Sunday had been outside the window, listening to Pauline sing. His eyes, full of that painful light, signified to Turner a touching belief in the possibilities of life, when God still inhabited this fresh green world, a last vestige of raw frontier innocence.

Turner had thought he was strong enough to journey again into Temple Woods, to face up to what he knew he would see and smell in there, to know the rough texture of the cold buttocks, the moment of penetration, then the strong animal smell that contaminates his own flesh, and gets into the grain of his skin so that no matter how hard he tries, he can never scrub it out again. Perhaps Robertson was right. Disease is retribution. But this contamination was different from the black diphtheria and other epidemics. It was altogether another order of defilement. Turner himself was part of that evil in the trees, the shivering tree-thing in her cloak of grass and owl feathers, her skin smeared dark with feces. Turner knew that he himself was tainted by that savagery. There was the stain of that primitive nightmare in Turner's own rioting heart.

Pauline narrowed her eyes, as though the mere mention of the boy's name caused her pain. "It seems that human nature doesn't have any way, except always to do the cruelest thing," she said. "I'm afraid I can't fully explain it to you. Except to say that I have some very good informants in the Spirit World."

"Well, the Spirit World is one thing. But is that evidence to hang a boy with? What makes you think he is still alive?"

Pauline lowered her voice and told him in a confidential tone that someone had come to her window in the night and shot at her piano. A hen had been nailed to the door of the barn the previous month. She was certain now that the culprit was Billy Sunday. And in the evenings now, when she sang, she was certain he was still out there, hiding, creeping through the darkness of the trees to listen to her voice, just as he used to stand outside the window. She felt his eyes on her, burning into her. How he stared! His little face with its smile of pain, bathed in the golden light of the righteous. She sensed that there was something terribly wrong with this boy. As she sang, she felt an invisible hand touch her, and move slowly down her body like icy fingers. Billy Sunday was still a presence here, in the trees, around the house at night, unheard, unseen, except for a single glimpse she had of him in the woods. She saw him standing there, stark naked, staring at her from the edge of the lake. Billy Sunday staring at her with those strange eyes. Him with his praying and his Bible.

She said she had not seen Billy Sunday after that. He must have gone back to hide in the forest, hearing those voices of his. There was Indian in him, after all, something cruel and secretive that always drew him back into the woods. The forest was his brother; its heart possessed the same kind of silence.

There was something else, Pauline said. Weeks earlier, during one of their sessions of spirit photography in the woods, Billy Sunday had turned up unexpectedly. He was wearing his satchel, as usual, that contained his Bible. He was very much disturbed about something. He was trembling, shaking. He would not look her in the eye. He complained of hearing voices whispering to him something he did not want to hear. Those voices tormented him, urging him to do all kinds of wicked things. "They tell me to lock the door," he said. "It is a building without windows. It is always night in there. It is the loneliest place in the world. There is a girl inside, and there is the smell of fish in there, the smell of rotting salmon." Those voices in his head were telling him that he ought to kill the girl.

That day in the woods he had said to Pauline, "Please make them stop, they are driving me to madness. I shall be obliged to you, Lady, if you would please make them stop."

That evening when Turner returned to the inn, he went straight into the drinking lounge, not having any fishing equipment to stow outside. A buzz of excitement animated the drinkers. Turner had already mounted the stairs to go to his room when his curiosity got the better of him. He went over to the group of men who had assembled around Robertson, whose face was even more flushed than usual. Turner could not at first understand what it was they were talking about. It fell to Robertson to break the news. "Go and have a look for yourself. No need to rush. She's not going anywhere. In fact, she's frozen stiff."

The body of a girl had been found in the ice shed behind the inn.

9

BILLY SUNDAY

RINGLING BROS.
WORLD'S GREATEST RAILROAD SHOW.
Great Triple Circus, Museum, Menagerie.
Universal World's Exposition.

The Indescribable, Tremendous Monster of Brute
Creation, the Largest Living Hippopotamus in
captivity. Sumatran Rhinoceros, the Monster Blood-
Sweating Behemoth of Holy Writ. 250 head of horses,
200 star circus performers, 80 startling sensational acts,
75 eminent musicians. Five glorious bands of music.
Real Roman Hippodrome and Roman Pageant. Roman

Gala Day Sports and Spectacles. Athletic pastimes of
Ancient Ages. Spectacular Tournament. Production of
Caesar's Triumphal Entry into Rome.
Ringling Bros. Three-Ring Circus and Elevated Stages.
Millionaire Menagerie, Museum and Aquarium.

PRESENTING

BUFFALO BILL

(himself) Col. Wm. Cody, Perils and Privations of
Pioneer Days. Pageant and the 101 Ranch Shows
Combined. Gorgeously picturesque frontier parade.
2 miles of strenuous movement & radiating color.

AND IN CONTINUOUS EXHIBITION . . .

WONDERWORLD

Van Amburgh's Great Golden Menagerie. Daredevils,
the Human Cannonball, Lulu the Man. Nero the
Untameable. The Bower of Beauty, 40 beautiful young
ladies, Nymphs of the Air.

THE CONGRESS OF FREAKS

Signor Pietro D'Olivera with his 200 white rats. The
Texas Fat Girl, Mountain of Flesh, Alice from Dallas,
at 685 pounds. And . . . Albinos, Armless Persons,
Bearded Women, Bird Circuses, Double-Bodied
Person, Dwarfs, The Elephant Boy, Fire-Eaters, Giants,
the Giraffe-Necked Burmese, Glass-blowers, Hawaiian
Dancers, The Human Pincushion, Hypnotists,

Illusionists, Knife and Tomahawk Throwers, Legless
Persons, The Living Skeleton, Magicians, Midgets
Aplenty, Mind-Readers, Ossified Men, Pinheads,
Rubberskins, the Saucer-Lipped Ubangis, Siamese
Twins, Snake Charmers, Sword-Swallowers, Tattoo
Man, Translucent Persons, Two-Headed Persons,
Ventriloquists, Wild Men of Borneo. And presenting
the Psychic Marvel and Clairvoyant, Dr. Anfin, the
New Necromancer. Sees, Knows & Tells All.
Like a bridge of dreams, the circus connects
youth with old age.

Purchase yr. tickets from our bulletproof, burglarproof ticket wagon.

ADULTS 50 CENTS.
CHILDREN UNDER 12, 25 CENTS.

Note: Owing to an agreement of the American
Showmen's Pooled League Association, this will be the
only Big Show to visit north Wisconsin this year.

On the train, Billy Sunday watched the faces of the circus
people, and those of the poor creatures who followed the
circus, clung to the cars and hid on the roof in the hope of
being given work, the women with ragged faces who sat on
their cases, eyes just staring.

The more privileged members of the circus went to sleep
in their carriages, and some time in the night they would
waken with a jolt as the rail cars were coupled and then,
some time later, they would be dreamily aware of the fact of

motion, the rhythm of the pushing steam. Some of the carriages were just ordinary boxcars, while others had been built like cages. On the open cars he saw the brightly painted steam calliope and the bell wagon.

In the morning, laborers were already at work. The Superintendent of Canvas, Jim Whalen, was overseeing the loading onto the baggage horses, of which there were three hundred. The circus was to be held at the fairgrounds on the edge of town, where the wooden, steam-driven Ferris wheel had already been erected. Later that morning, when the tent had been prepared, there was a street parade down Main Street to attract customers to the show at seven in the evening. In the windows of the stores were the lithograph posters with date sashes promising all the Ringling Brothers had to offer.

First came the Columbia Band Wagon, with its beautifully carved faces of women and angels, golden hair streaming back behind, eyes staring ahead to their destiny. The great bell wagon came next, here in its first season. Cage-carts followed, and when one of the lions snarled, the edge of the crowd quickly moved back. Here were the famous performers from the Ringling Brothers Circus, who before today had been remote and romantic figures on the posters. It was amazing that there on Main Street was Bird Millman, the tightrope walker, and Jules Tournier, the clown. Next came the forty-horse wagon, then the tableau wagons, each drawn by twenty horses. The last wagon in the street parade was the steam calliope, and its music lived on in the ears of the spectators, during the inevitable sadness when the parade had finished.

In the evening, even before the gas lamps were lit, people walked through the muddy streets past the store windows and the drinking lounges. Throngs of bright-faced people were already headed toward the fairgrounds, looking for adventure.

The crowds lined up at the ticket wagon. People liked to stroll for an hour or so along the sideshow alleys before the start of the show under the big top. They filled the sideshow alleys, the little tents of vendors of all manner of unusual things, the dingy tents with crap games, the shooting galleries. They passed the freak show tents and the duck boards set up in front where the strange menagerie was paraded for the edification of a curious public—the bone man, Mr. Ricks; the Siamese Twins. They passed tents where horoscopes were cast and dreams interpreted, where the "gypsy" fortune teller, Madame Babylon, gazed into her crystal ball to read the future and the past.

The House of the Bible had been devised by Mr. Otto Ringling as a way of appeasing those Temperance Union ladies who had been so troublesome lately. They claimed the circus brought immorality into their towns, and that the liquor tents turned their husbands into carousers. He did not expect it to be a great success. After all, he reasoned, who would attend the Bible tent, when men had the Bower of Beauty to feast their eyes on?

Those temperance ladies need not have worried. It soon became apparent they would require a bigger tent for "the Bible show." The tent they had been using accommodated two dozen people at most. In the new tent they installed long planks which seated sixteen people across. From some distance away, the sound of the audience praying could be heard.

The route book of the Ringling Brothers Circus showed the dates the circus would be in each town that year. The circus traveled through the countryside all summer, then returned to its winter quarters at Baraboo. Each year the circus was equipped with new tents. At the end of each summer in Baraboo all the ropes and canvas from that year were sold to local farmers, under the supervision of Jim Whalen, Superintendent of Canvas.

It was the end of three days of rain at Baraboo. Billy Sunday could hear the dull thuds from the barn of the other workers beating and folding the canvas that was to be sold at auction the following week. Ten minutes later, they too had finished work and he heard someone crossing the yard.

Now the door opened and it was Madame Babylon. She was an old, old woman. When she came to him, her old sun-wrinkled face was a cobweb of lines, and seemed to confirm her claim that she was a hundred years old. She stood in the doorway, looking around Billy Sunday's squalid room, the strip of yellow rug, the worm-eaten table, the narrow cot against the wall.

He knew without asking why she had come. She had been waiting fifteen years for just this moment to begin her story. The moment her mouth opened and he heard her words, Billy Sunday felt the air in the room suddenly rush close by his head.

It was a tale, known to Madame Babylon alone, which she had shared with no one in the intervening years. She wanted to tell Billy Sunday what had happened to Lalla Rookh, who was billed as The Most Beautiful Woman in the World. She had been for a few months in late 1877 one of the original members of the Bower of Beauty, before the Ringlings, in the days of Orton's Old Badger Circus.

As she spoke, Madame Babylon's eyes were beautiful again, full of youth and light. The room filled with a haze of sunlight and a woman appeared just then like a vision of the Virgin Mary. It was his mother, Lalla Rookh. The skin of her face was so smooth he wanted to reach out and touch her cheek. "It's not right," he said. "You're still alive."

His mother stepped forward and put her arms around him. He felt such a sunny peace. He felt during that single touch made whole again, and felt the burden of his pain shrivel away through his flesh. He was a part of the Holy Family, the child protected by both mother and father; the father not absconded; the mother not turned into a whore; the child not put away into an orphanage run by the Wisconsin Benevolent Society. She let him forget about time. The defeat set in the bones of his face was soothed away. She showed him parish papers of his birth and baptism in the name of Billy Sunday because that was the day of the week he had been born on. Time was saturated by her talk. She told him how she had felt when he was six weeks old, when she had wrapped him up in his blanket and looked upon him for the last time, before she had given him up for Madame Babylon to place in an orphanage. She told him about her life in the Bower of Beauty, and how she had fallen under the shadow of the Old Necromancer, who had long since departed the circus.

The parish papers she was holding contained a folded drawing, and he could make out in the lines of the rough sketch a baby's face. The day before she was due to give him up, she had asked one of the circus artists, who sketched a person's likeness in two minutes for ten cents, to draw her baby so that she could have something to remember him by. She had seen only limitless time stretching ahead into the future, frozen wastes of a life, the tundra of dead feeling. In that numbness and despair in the hours after she had given up her baby, she had set off like a lost explorer who, instead of suicide, continues on a hopeless journey to a future she had no faith in finding.

The notes of her music nibbled through the walls of his harsh young life. He allowed himself to take refuge in this joyful vision, for the thing that had brought him to this state of comfort, half asleep, mildly caressing himself, was being able to see for the first time an image of his mother, Lalla Rookh, The Most Beautiful Woman in the World, lying on a silk divan, the jewel of the Bower of Beauty, wearing nothing but her dancing tights and Turkish slippers.

Billy Sunday was unaware of the minutes ticking away as he floated in that sunny peace, until the cruel moment when rational thought returned to him and the ice of time hardened in his heart again. The old woman was still sitting in his room, still talking. Her ugly old stomach hung through her dress where her corsets had burst. He said to her, "Where's Mother?"

"She's not far away," came the answer. Then she added in a whisper, "In the Spirit World."

She sat and spoke for hour after hour, and while he sat and listened with his face full of pain, Billy Sunday was already looking ahead in time to that distant day when he would escape the circus, and the tyranny of Mr. Whalen, Superintendent of Canvas. He could already look ahead and see his own tracks in life being covered by snow, forgotten. His old life, all that had taken place in the forest, and afterward, the girl he had seen in the lake, might be forgotten, too.

After all these years, the people were so remote, but they were still alive in Madame Babylon's mind. When the old woman had finished telling Billy Sunday, he continued to see it in such a vivid and detailed way, as if it were all still happening somewhere in the present. He kept his mother's picture in his mind, having her adjust her beautiful long black hair, or the gesture of her hand; then he saw himself crouch behind the black hood of the camera on its wooden legs to take the picture. Everyone else had parents. He now had Lalla Rookh. Her lovely face still hovered in the room, ghostly, luminous. He did not allow himself to sleep, nor to count the hours until it would be morning and he would have to work again, the hours of ropes and canvas, aching wrists and fingers. Her image would be absorbed by the sunlight.

While the music of his own story echoed in his soul, quite another chord had begun to reverberate in his mind. There had been others, Madame Babylon had said, who had been seduced and abandoned by the Old Necromancer over the years. She remembered one young girl, a child they had called "Pauline the German," a singer whose voice even then was so pure it soared up into the sky. Such a superb voice might have made her into a famous singer in the opera, had it not been for her misfortune, and the Old Necromancer's perfidy.

After all that passage of time, Madame Babylon could not forget the effect the Old Necromancer had on her. "Even if he was in the same room, I felt myself choking and I had to go outside to get some fresh air," she said. The Old Necromancer had left the circus many years ago, now. His place had been taken by another showman, Dr. Anfin, the New Necromancer. Occasionally there were reports of an itinerant mesmerist at one or another place in the wilderness. There were other rumors, too, about a young man who bore an uncanny resemblance to the Old Necromancer, and who had been following girls in country towns across the state, the past two years.

The Old Necromancer had appeared every night before his audience with a solemn face, his glowing forehead made more prominent by his receding hair. He was proud and patrician in his bearing, notwithstanding his crude outbursts of anger. Even though he claimed he was of noble birth in Russia, and spoke with the stage voice of an actor, deep and melodious, like the lower stop on an organ, he would suddenly round upon them, boiling with abuse, too completely eaten up by his anger to effectively hit or kick them. He looked as though he was about to vomit.

Very few people even knew what his real name was. He kept himself aloof, as tall and gaunt as an undertaker in his morning coat. Something must have happened to him when he was young to have soured his character. He was abusive with subordinates, and everyone was frightened of him. He was the most unhappy man in the world. Once, flying into a rage with one of the girls who featured in his act, he nearly took her eyes out. He did not just give her a bit of a slap, the way you do with a silly girl, but flew at her face with his fingernails in a murderous rage. He fought the way a wild animal does, or a woman.

The Old Necromancer stayed up late into the night, his oil lamp lit and his blanket around his shoulders, poring over his books of alchemy and hypnosis. He had once been director of a morgue, and, by his own account at least, had by the proximity to so many corpses discovered his ability in necromancy. When he had gone upon the stage he continued to dress in the manner of his former vocation, as a mortician. He made a good impression on stage with his English manners and fine clothes, starched collars, silk waistcoat, his morning suit always impeccably pressed.

He could be seen peeking from behind the curtain before each performance, counting the heads. On stage he commanded real presence. He spoke with a magnificent formality in his deep, Russian voice. He was one of those men who live more in their own world than in the rough commerce of their fellow citizens. His voice was pleasant, sonorous, so deep it took the listener far away. People said it was like his voice gave off a secret perfume that lulled and enchanted, that took them to a place where a beautiful light existed, far into the future, a world where the light shone through the dust of their own bones. His audience never suspected that he might be guilty of perfidious conduct.

Madame Babylon was frightened of him. His world contained the sudden violence of a dream. At times it seemed that there were other personalities working through the muscles of his face, transforming him. Those eyes of his were burning like coals, and it seemed that he was driven by some terrible desire.

To touch that cold hand of his and to look into his eyes was like falling down a dark precipice. As soon as he began speaking with his lovely voice, the air grew thick with brown smoke. Few people, even among the hardened professionals of the circus, knew his tricks. Some said that he really did possess the powers of necromancy. He would take on the physical form of the soul who was talking through him. He would swagger around the stage for a long time before he felt the kick of another spirit enter him. On occasion he would even reenact the scenes of death, the kick of a horse, or vomiting, in the throes of some self-administered poison. Or, making an accusation about a member of the audience by name, he rolled around the floor, shouting in a croaky voice that was not his own that he had been poisoned, rat poison was the culprit. Someone had tampered with the town's supply of cocaine, poisoned it with strychnine, but Mr. Olsen, the druggist, was not to blame. Then he would take advantage of the ensuing tumult to dramatic effect.

"Keep your children away! Keep your children away from the Necromancer when he is in his trance!" shouted Clifford Bell, the Negro attaché.

But still the Old Necromancer remained in his trance, filling himself with the voices of the lost souls. His eyes turned back in their sockets, and he lost consciousness, frothing at the mouth.

At one time, it became known that the Old Necromancer and his assistant were not getting along. They could be heard from their wagon, squabbling like turkeys. Through the open door of his wagon, that famous trunk of his could be seen, fitted with a stout hasp, padlocked.

Once, when Madame Babylon had passed his wagon, he had been preparing himself for a bath, heating water for his hip bath on the same little oil stove he used for his alchemy. Watching him through the window of the wagon, she had seen him turned in the middle of his ablutions and he seemed neither man nor woman completely. She saw the plump incipient breasts, the pubic patch which concealed his genitalia. And the Old Necromancer was sometimes seen in the company of an effeminate man, Dr. Pietro D'Olivera, the keeper of two hundred albino rats.

Some claimed the Old Necromancer had the beginnings of wings on his back. Others had claimed that he was unable to consummate any of his conquests with women, as he had been born without a penis, or that his penis was too small to perform the act. But it was only his human presence that was devoid of masculinity. It might have been the Old Necromancer himself who had spread the rumor that when he was with a woman he became the incarnate shade of a hanged man, who had a monstrous masculinity, and who returned to deal retribution to the woman who had unfairly accused him in life.

He always spent the greater part of each day alone, carrying on his "psychic research." He used to say that Nature is the basis of all religion, and he often used to go off into the woods alone, wherever the circus happened to be, walk to the edge of the town and just keep on walking. He always came back by show time, though. He was very professional like that.

Everyone in the circus soon knows everyone else's business, their professional secrets, how they do their tricks; but not with him. There were people who said they were not sideshow tricks at all, but genuine acts of Black Magic and that the Necromancer was really a witch. He had his own wagon, all to himself, all French-polished wood and velvet curtains, and his faithful assistant, Clifford Bell. People said, who knows? Maybe the Necromancer has him in a spell, too? His air of obsessive secrecy, his love of secrets, his violent accusations that somebody had been getting into his trunk while he was out, all had the effect of making everyone wonder just what it was he kept in his trunk that he wanted to keep so secret.

Lalla Rookh had emerged from the Bower of Beauty wearing a sari of shot silk in shimmering peacock greens and blues. She walked through the still night, with the rain in her hair, that magnificent black hair always groomed with golden pins and combs. Her wet hair, close around her head, accentuated her beauty. She had been elevated immediately to the Bower of Beauty.

Lalla Rookh! Departure from Delhi to the Vale of Cashmere!

Famed as the World's Most Beautiful Woman!

The Old Necromancer told her she had that fresh, newly minted quality of youth, the kind of beauty that when a man sees her for the first time he feels his heart stop; then his blood hammering through him again like a rabbit in fright. He told her that the moment he had seen her in the Bower of Beauty he knew he was changed forever. He had walked from that moment forth in a cocoon of new feeling. He felt a tenderness for her, as if they had been born of the same blood, and only they could know it. All he wanted in the world now was to give her pleasure. All of which perhaps was not too great an exaggeration. He had walked through those first days in a kind of worship of her.

So corrupt was the Old Necromancer in his art that Billy's mother was not his only girlfriend. He had simultaneously engaged the affections of several girls from the Bower of Beauty. This was not due to good looks or charm, nor even to that commanding presence of his on the stage; but was due to the fact that nearly everyone had a loved one gone to the Spirit World, and through the medium of this tall, gloomy man, sought to make contact with the departed souls. In return, some women would allow him to perform those carnal acts they would allow some other man to perform on them on a Saturday night anyway, and which many of them had done for a dollar a trick, in tough periods of their lives.

Lalla Rookh's parents had been killed when she was a

child, and she had been raised by an older brother. When Lalla Rookh had gone one night to the Old Necromancer's wagon to speak with the spirits of her dead parents, he had raised his face to her, a slight smile on his lips, and in the lamplight his face seemed bathed in the sublime pleasure she had seen on those who had taken opium.

In spite of the solemnity with which the Old Necromancer had prepared the opium pipes for the seance, Lalla Rookh had responded to his invitation to smoke by shrieking with laughter. She was so frightened, there was the same feeling of a live creature gnawing through her guts she remembered when she had suffered from diarrhea.

Then, as she had sucked the sweet smoke of paradise deep into her lungs, she found herself surrounded by whispers. The whispering voices seemed to be everywhere, coming from all directions in the air. They came from the soft nap of the oriental cushions, from the wood-paneled walls themselves. It was as though the spirits had been injected into her veins and rode their lovely race through her limbs.

Those whispering spirits ate at the silence. She heard the whoosh of suddenly escaping air. But even as they swooped and soared around her, something kept a steady chord, a woman's voice it might have been, or the wavering breath of the *vox angelica* on an organ. The whispering air grew suddenly louder, like the roaring of flames. Her mother was speaking to her from her funeral pyre.

It might have been the unaccustomed luxury of the feather bed, but she had fallen effortlessly to sleep in the Necromancer's wagon, and when she awoke, the whispering air was shredded to the shrieking of birds and the light of dawn was creeping over the sky in the east. She woke to find herself naked in the Necromancer's bed, with its silk cushions, his luxurious damask cloak spread across her. She remembered then that during the night the Old Necromancer had made of her his natural wife.

The Necromancer had undressed her, opened her sari, marveling at her fine shoulders, the petals of her breasts. Her sleeping body seemed to fill with fresh new life at every breath. Her hard little belly was slightly swollen, like that of a girl a couple of months pregnant. Such was her beauty that he was aching instantly to penetrate her. He knew he had to violate her virtue, to taste of that divine body. Though Lalla Rookh was billed on the circus posters as The Most Beautiful Woman in the World, the slim, tobacco-skinned girl who lay before him was a creature too fabulous for an overused word like "beauty." She had long black hair that reached down to the backs of her thighs and the movement of her buttocks like sliding silk cushions bewitched him, seduced him. He looked down at her long legs, her slim ankles. The silver bangles on her wrists were even more exciting, now that she was naked. And there was something else, unusual in a girl from Cashmere, a small tattoo of the head of a jaguar on her upper arm, just below the shoulder.

He had raped Lalla Rookh that night, Lalla Rookh with her long black hair, and her eyes that had been hidden by her peaceful, perfect eyelids. And once, during the moment of delight, when the fireworks were going off in his body, he looked down and saw the startled light, the wonder in her eyes, as she woke from her trance, suddenly puzzled by the new breathing so close to her, the harsh noise of his boiling breath on her face; then immediately began to struggle and panic. She had been dreaming of the Vale of Cashmere, yet here she was in Orton's Old Badger Circus, waking under the weight of a stranger. She tried to scream, but the Old Necromancer placed his hand softly over her mouth; a signal to her of what might come, rather than any physical coercion. Yet there was contained in that slight pressure on her throat the threat of much, much more.

Her frightened eyes appealed to any trace of pity that remained in his heart. But the Old Necromancer's heart was made of flint; and every act of love he performed was an attempt to cure his affliction. The Necromancer, without a twinge of conscience, had promised himself to her. It would come to seem incomprehensible to Lalla Rookh that the Necromancer was enamored of her, so crudely and brutally did he treat her. But the invasion of her body was only a prelude to the occupation of her soul, where he continued to lurk in the weeks ahead.

To Lalla Rookh's consternation, there were evenings when the Old Necromancer would not admit her to his wagon, and she could not get past his assistant, Clifford Bell.

He did not look at her for days on end. She bore up under her ordeal, and it was only during the course of the following weeks that she discovered that the Old Necromancer was so practiced in his art as a mesmerist, that many of the others from the Bower of Beauty had woken on the silk and damask pillows of the Necromancer's bed.

She watched half the night, until she saw him finally return to the wagon with another of the girls from the Bower of Beauty. What would the girl think when Lalla Rookh told her that *she* had already been promised the Necromancer as a husband? The Old Necromancer had impaled her, like a roast turkey.

Lalla Rookh said it wasn't right for a gentleman to breach his promise, and she threatened to write to the President about it. But she did not reveal to him that night, nor on any subsequent night, the secret that had made her run away from home and join the circus. She kept that secret closely guarded. She did not reveal to him that there was a solid lump of flesh already growing in her womb.

Nor did she reveal it, at first, to the other girls in the Bower of Beauty; until their arrival in Baraboo with Christmas snow, and it was during this festive season that Madame Babylon had first noticed the five-month swelling under her sari, as much as the desperation that had begun to harden the muscles in her lovely face.

Mr. Jim Whalen, Superintendent of Canvas, a stout, stern Scot with thick corded arms like the ropes and knots he was also Superintendent of, was informed of most things that went on in the circus. He was an old hand who had worked in Orton's Old Badger Circus too, and he liked to know the personal business of everyone in his employ. He had heard about Madame Babylon's visit to Billy Sunday, and summoned the boy to his office. His mouth was kind under his big mustache as the boy told his story.

"My God. You're Lalla's boy. You're nothing like her,

except for the dark skin in you. But your resemblance to *him* is uncanny. I daresay there's a good deal of immorality attached to circus people. It goes with the life. In all my years as Superintendent of Canvas, I've never met an Indian who could do an honest day's work like you can. Yes, my boy, you're half Indian, all right. But you've got the wrong India. Lalla Rookh wouldn't have known the Vale of Cashmere if she fell down it. Lalla Rookh was just a stage name, anyway. She was a pureblood Winnebago princess. But think about it, Billy, any way you like. You've got thief in your blood. You may be half the wrong kind of Indian. You're Lalla's boy, all right. But you're also the son of the Old Necromancer. He and Clifford Bell disappeared the night the strongbox was robbed, that strongbox kept chained to the floor of the ticket wagon. You got thief in you. It's not your fault, but it's right there in your blood until the day you die, and there's nothing anybody can do about it. It ain't fair and all that, but you was born with a curse and there's no end to it." Then Jim Whalen's face softened. "Lalla Rookh! She was only with the circus for a few months, then the winter here in Baraboo, before she had her baby. Everyone blamed the Old Necromancer, but who knows? Lots of young girls get pregnant and run away from home to join the circus."

Billy Sunday could think of nothing else. The train of memory would not stop at the stations of the ordinary working day. He stood for minutes, his hands idle on the ropes, his gaze abstracted. He saw clearly again the events which had befallen Lalla Rookh at the hands of the Old Necromancer. Slats of light fell across his face and he swayed with the motion of the Old Necromancer's wagon, heard the creaking of the wood-paneled walls, and saw the piles of damask cushions and the beautiful girl waking up in the dawn light. He saw the ghost of Lalla Rookh and behind her the figure of his father. He had found not a hook to hang his name on, but rather the tail end of something, a land of shadows he was exiled from, and allowed only vivid, puzzling glimpses, as in dreams. He realized that until he had traced the spoor of the Old Necromancer he would not have finished his journey.

The Nymphs of the Air trained in the Bower of Beauty with an inflexible discipline, hour after hour on the trapeze and the Roman rings. As he watched trapeze practice that afternoon, Billy Sunday felt an unspoken hostility toward him on the part of the performers, as if by now they too all knew his secret. He was the son of the Old Necromancer. He had the same stain on his soul.

When Billy Sunday was paid, he went to one of the women who followed the circus around from town to town, who pitched their tents a little distance away and lay there waiting, with their rags and fleas, for customers, or for the Pinkertons hired by the circus to move them on. Now in winter, they lived in rooms above a bar in Baraboo. She was not beautiful, like Lalla Rookh had been. But it didn't matter.

It was midwinter in Baraboo, the quietest time of the year. The Baraboo River was frozen, a deep cover of snow blanketed the ground and hushed the world. All was silent during the days, except that sometimes from the direction of one of the houses would come the harsh insistent scraping of a shovel clearing snow from a path or doorway.

Billy Sunday examined his face in the mirror, scanning it for traces of criminality. He tried to read the map of lines on his forehead, his eyes driven into his head at a sharp angle. He tried to imagine a Russian version of his own face, its features slightly distorted, as though an invisible thumb had just smudged it, fattened the lips and shortened the nose, closed up the eyes. His hair was cropped close to his skull like a convict, emphasizing the protruding ball of the forehead, the Asiatic eyes. His skin was pale, dry and papery, almost translucent. Billy Sunday looked back at that stranger's face. He felt that same quicksilver of fear as when he had found that girl in the woods, rotted into the dark floor of the forest, the soft skin of compost covering her. He had seen that frightening face in one of Mr. Van Schaick's photographic plates last summer. It was the face of one who had given in to temptation again and again.

Billy Sunday wobbled the glass slightly and watched the face transform back and forth from the other to his own. Then he turned the mirror sideways, and the steady line of the eyes stared back at him, hard, unflinching, as emotionless as objects. But it was no good. They were someone else's eyes; not his. Someone who belonged to another people. They could not have been his father's eyes.

He heard the clock ticking fast like a metronome, and time reversed its course for him and he went back to the place in his life where the river had been damned and the waters had spread out over the fields, drowning feeling. Billy Sunday could not stop the loud ticking in his ears.

Then he felt another face come close to him, a weird face, but also a deeply comforting face, like a grandfather's: a face which knew him. He could smell the squirrel meat on its breath. He could feel the thick lips part and blow tobacco smoke on him, initiate him, anoint him.

Lalla Rookh had not needed to listen for very long to the stories of the Old Necromancer's countless affairs; and about those other engagements of his which had been announced, only to be discreetly withdrawn later. Only now did Lalla Rookh understand the meaning of the marks she had seen on his wall above the headboard of the bed. Hers were the tears of a girl who realized she would never be able to marry now. She had reduced herself to a whore.

Lalla Rookh asked only that she be left alone with her humiliation. Then people began to notice that Lalla Rookh was kind of languid all the time. A funny thing. Her fingernails turned bright yellow. People said when they saw those sad, heavy-lidded eyes of hers that she was taking too many doses of opium. One night, the girls of the Bower of Beauty were woken by the sound of someone vomiting. It wasn't opium Lalla Rookh had been taking, but salts of strychnine. She hoped it might rid her of the homunculus who, even now, was spreading his icy fingers through her stomach.

The night she sent for her seducer, she wore a nightgown to cover the shape of her body. The Old Necromancer arrived in his plush smoking jacket, alone, a scowl on his face, for he had a gloomy and private disposition when he was off the stage. He kept his moral ledger in the same way that some men keep a daily balance sheet of their household expenses. He decided that it was unreasonable for him to deprive himself of his liberty just because he had taken the girl a few times. And he concluded, furthermore, that it would have been indelicate to discuss the matter with her. She had wanted to throw herself over the edge of the Falls, but at the final moment, she had held herself off the lovers' leap, out of pity for the soul of her unborn baby.

By the time she was dismissed from the circus, Lalla Rookh was already a changed person. Thinking about how things had worked out, she felt a bitter pleasure in sacrificing her youthful beauty that had aroused so many men. Well, now they would have to be content with souvenir postcards of her. Her famous face had dried up, her skin grown slack, so that the habitual expression she wore now was the impassive look of old squaws who had sat out in the sun for too many years.

The Old Necromancer had already fled Baraboo, the town where he had undertaken too many faithless loves. His train had passed the auction rooms at the winter quarters where they sold the ropes and canvas to the farmers. The railroad line through the swamp led away to where the Old Necromancer might again satisfy his wild longings. That had been the day the strongbox was robbed, and he had just vanished, and Clifford Bell, too, not even coming back for his stage clothes.

Pain coiled inside her and she knew it would soon be night. Dreaded night. Every night now she dreamed of a jaguar inching toward her through the trees. When she woke, she could still hear its snarling.

She stood at the window of her room above a saloon, as night crept over the street, and the shape of the dream animal moved over her face. It came upon her just then, without warning. The jaguar head of the Manitouiriniou appeared and smiled at her, told her in her own language that it was time, and already she was screaming out. Somehow the baby was already slipping out of her. She pushed the glutinous egg back up between her thighs and tried to walk. Screaming. Then she was bending over, tugging at the slippery thing between her legs and putting it in the chamber pot, but it was still attached to her, pulling out the thread of her own insides. She picked up the bread knife, she didn't have time to lie down on the bed, she touched the shoulder of the egg, then traced its root, she did not scream, she smiled and cut. "So you are here," she said to the object in the chamber pot. The object that, to her puzzlement, was moving.

Now she lifted it from the chamber pot, his face already screwed up and reddened with rage. He was surprisingly heavy, and she could hardly keep her fingers from sinking into him. The tiny slitted eyes were open, and he blindly cast his gaze at her. She tried to close the miniature eyes as best she could.

All through the Sunday night of the birth, Lalla Rookh kept her secret in the bed with her. Instead of happiness, there was a taste of poison in the room. Billy Sunday, base-born in a prostitute's room to the most beautiful woman in the Bower of Beauty, burst from his mother's womb into the world bawling, strong as a tiger. He was already caught in the river of life, his heart beating strongly over rapids. And as his little face filled with blood, and as his mouth opened and his eyes slitted up with rage, he looked already wizened and old. He was born already old.

She determined that the Old Necromancer would never trace the child, and made arrangements through Madame Babylon for him to be taken to an orphanage in Milwaukee, with the promise of a decent Christian upbringing, away from the corrupting influences of the circus.

Six weeks later he was passing across a long wooden rail-road bridge over a frozen river, in Madame Babylon's arms. Dotted along the riverbank were the camps of gangs of tramps. Smoke rose from their bonfires on the dull, still, snow-hushed afternoon. Since many of the children in the orphanages were half-caste, she would not have been able to identify him. She could not reach him. He would have been given another name, his spirit already reaching out along the paths of life, searching for a lost thing. It would not be possible to find the child. Her signature on the document was duly witnessed. She made it a condition that the child never be told the identity of his mother, nor of his supposed father, as if the mere knowledge of it would transmit to him the Necromancer's cursed heritage.

Lalla Rookh had come to expect men to use her to satisfy their carnal appetites. Going to live in the prostitutes' quarters above the saloon in Baraboo, she hardly cared whether there was a man inside her or not. She had scars on her upper arms from men's teeth. The row of plaster saints on the shelf above her bed looked down upon her, the Holy Family in their biblical robes the muted tones of deep rose and blue-grey. Their gentle expressions showed compassion for all that was enacted there.

In the end, Lalla Rookh dressed and made her way to the train station in Baraboo and waited, ashamed, in the back alley with the freight, the hay bales, crates of oranges and cans of kerosene. The train she took traveled in the opposite direction to Milwaukee. It followed the Soo Line to the north of the state, to the forests on the shores of Lake Superior.

Madame Babylon had never seen Lalla Rookh again after that, though she had later heard through another medium that Lalla Rookh had died by her own hand, and that she had gone across to the Spirit World.

Boys from the town liked to hang around the winter quarters of the circus, in a bend of the Baraboo River, with all its associations of carefree days. They could watch the trains pass from there. On that day, Madame Babylon had stood outside the circus compound with the boys playing and watched the smoke from her train drifting where the sun was low and red, at six o'clock in the afternoon.

———

At this point, the engine of memory gathered its own steam. Billy Sunday still remembered well the grey face of the director, Dr. Nathaniel Shaw, a man given to bouts of religious mania and violent temper, who induced into his charges a fear of God through daily Bible readings and some six-foot reins he kept specifically for their chastisement.

The Wisconsin Benevolent Society was funded by its benefactors on the condition that its charges kept the Protestant faith. Life at the orphanage came to a sudden halt at the age of twelve. Recruiters from the logging camps called at the orphanage each year on the first of May, and took away those boys who in the last year had turned twelve, to work, when the rivers had thawed, in the wanigans, the floating cookhouses on the rivers, which followed the logs downriver to the mills and ships each summer. In winter they holed up in the frozen camps with violent men, whose only outlet was a night out in the nearest town. There they fought with men from the other camps and timber mills, the bull-buckers, cat-skinners and boomers. The lumberjacks' Saturday night invasions of these north woods towns were notorious. It was said that the four toughest places in the world were Cumberland, Hayward, Hurley and Hell.

This was the burden of injustice and hate that Billy Sunday had carried around with him during those years, learning to fight with a knife in the logging camps, protecting himself from queer cooks in the wanigans. He had seen more than one man with his skull busted with a blackjack. Once he had done it himself with a tent peg. A tramp had started to fight and Billy Sunday had picked up an iron peg and dug the hooked end in and that was that.

All the hateful experience in his young life, that had until now only been assuaged by reading the Bible, by a town photographer's kindness and by the divine voice of a visiting lady, now had a face.

He could already see the Old Necromancer tramping through the snowy woods. As he walked, his face was raised, transfixed by something just above the tree line. Billy Sunday felt he was high above the woods, he could look down and see the Old Necromancer down there, a ragged creature fleeing for its life. The fugitive was getting smaller all the time, a tiny figure in the great forest in the snow, the dark trees like fur upon the white land. The forgetful expanses of time stretched behind him.

He would track the Old Necromancer to wherever he was now and hack the life out of him.

10

FREDERICK JACKSON TURNER

That first journey he made to Balsam Point with his father in 1877 was the start of everything. Fred Turner would always remember his first sight of the north country, the train clattering along its narrow corridor through the trees, the great walls of the forest towering up on both sides. His father was involved in some land speculations in the pineries, business which had required his presence in the forests around Balsam Point for four months in the summer of 1877, and it was the most natural thing in the world for Andrew Jackson Turner to take along his fifteen-year-old son, Fred, who shared his ardent love of fly-fishing.

Every morning Fred would set off along the trail with his fly-rod and his rucksack with his lunch and walk to the trout streams in the hemlock woods behind the Indian mission. He met some of the local boys. They teased young "Portage," as they called him, about his fancy fly-fishing. They used worms, salmon eggs, goldenrod galls, Mayfly nymphs and perch eyes for bait. They had never cast dry flies before. They could not see any reason for giving the trout a chance. They sprinkled cornmeal on the surface to get the fish to rise.

Fred taught the other boys how to tie their own lures, the intricate, pretty little flies with the cruel barb hidden inside. He showed them how to tie a Red Hackle, with two fluffy red feathers from under a rooster's wattles; a McGinty with the feathers of goose, mallard duck and ostrich. He showed them how to tie a Hornberg Special and a red and black Cockabondy. There was even friendly competition between them. "You wait 'til tomorrow, Portage, then you'll see a trout," Jake boasted.

"Five pounder?"

"Sure. Why not a five pounder?"

"If it's that five pounder you're talking about," said Fred, "he's already mine."

The other boys were older, and knew more about the world. They had mixed with the wild men from the logging camps and timber mills. They knew how to hold their whiskey, and what to do with girls.

He slipped out of the leather straps of the knapsack and set it down against the trunk of a tree. He undid the buckle and took out his bread and cheese, the water bottle and the tin cup. The afternoon was hot, the leaves of the birch trees shimmering. There was the tinge of burning in the air, maybe from the loggers, or from the Indian mission.

"Hello there, Portage." Jake Rhinelander had already been drinking, and he was carrying the whiskey bottle by the neck. The white, sickly face smiled down at Fred. Jake pushed the bottle into his hand and gestured for him to drink. Fred pulled out the cork and took a long drink. Fred could feel his Adam's apple working up and down. The liquor burned in his throat.

He lay there on the pine needles, sweating. He could hear the nervous lapping of water at the lake. The pine branches swayed. Fred felt disappointed; hardly drunk at all, except for a slight dizziness, which he decided to exaggerate by holding his arms out and turning clockwise, making the trees and river appear again and again, until he dropped to his knees laughing and was swallowed up by the grass.

Soon Jake came along to find him. Jake's face seemed different, somehow. His eyes seemed clearer, bluer in his head and his breath came slow and noisy. Jake asked him if he'd remembered to bring his dollar.

"What do we need with a dollar up here?" Fred asked him.

The other brother, Moses, said, "That's what the bitch is for."

"What's it like, when you're with a woman?" Turner's heart began to pound.

Moses said carefully, "Well, it's the loneliest feeling in the world."

"Does it feel nice?" the boy asked.

"Well, you've been closer than anything else in life to her. Then, after you spend yourself out, you're back in yourself again, thinking why don't I feel so close to her anymore. Yes sir, it's lonely."

"She'll do it when she's ripe," Jake assured him.

"And how do you tell when she's ripe?" Fred demanded.

Jake said, "Well, it's a feeling. And, you can tell by the little man in the boat." Fred could only think of the painting in his mother's parlor, a boat in a storm in Maine tilted up at an angle in the violent light. The fisherman in his sou'wester bravely held on in the waves of brown-red sea.

"Does it feel nice?" he asked.

"It's always nice," said Jake. "What's the matter?"

"I don't know," Fred said and looked away.

"Oh hell, Portage. You ain't going to pull out of it now?"

"But couldn't we just go away? Wouldn't that make it all right?"

"Sure, Portage."

"I'm sure if we just went, it would turn out all right."

"We each pay our dollar. You promised me, hear?"

They waited in their underwear on the lake shore for the girl to come. The trees around them began to sway in the wind. Their underwear had darkened with wet patches, as though some dark substance was sweating out of their bodies. She finally turned up.

Jenny Four-Fingers watched him pour whiskey into the tin cup. She reached out and drank it all down. She did not show any ill effects from the liquor. After ten minutes, she lay down on the ground. "Only not the other one," she said. "He's too young. I don't go with him."

"You squaw," Jake said. "You'll go with whoever we say."

She said, "I don't go with him, definitely."

"You'll go with him, all right."

"Oh no," she said. But there was something in her voice that was already resigned to it.

"It's quite all right," Fred said. "Actually I don't terribly want to do it."

Her eyes looked back at him without expression, as though all men were alike to her and she didn't much care after all who this particular one happened to be. Then, without bothering to remove her boots, Jenny Four-Fingers lay on her back with her knees bent and her dark skirt pulled up to reveal plump thighs, and began moaning as soon as Jake had mounted her. She made a whimpering, insistent noise deep in her throat. Each boy had his turn with her in the trees.

Fred sat by himself against a tree in the peaceful sunny air and watched. For a long time, he simply sat there, unable to think anything at all. He felt himself to be at an incalculable distance, as if he were merely observing the scene as the weird and inexplicable actions of another race of creatures entirely. They were joined together only in the coercion of muscle and their harsh rhythmic breathing. He heard her say, "Hurry up. I want you to shoot. I haven't got all day."

Afterward, when Jake Rhinelander came across to get him, he saw that something had changed inside Fred. "Jesus,"

Fred said. He could not understand how the girl could allow such a thing to be done to her. His eyes were redrimmed. What Fred had witnessed had wounded him.

"She's a whore," Jake said. "She's dirt. Any dog with a dollar can bury his bone in her. She's an Indian. None of them are any different." He turned, as though that was the last word on the subject.

He saw Jane Whitecloud for the first time coming along the trail in dungarees and a red plaid shirt, a man's felt hat pulled down over her eyes. At fifteen, she might have been a boy, except for the braid of glossy black hair that reached down to the backs of her thighs.

Of all the Indian girls, Jane was the quiet one, the beauty who did not go with boys. She lived alone with her brother. Her mother and father had been killed by loggers when she was still a small child. The girls in the Indian village had a reputation for immorality and a few of them were known even to have had illegitimate children. Jane Whitecloud refused the attentions of the young men who sought her out. Men were always wanting to give her money. But this new boy from Portage seemed different from the others.

"They told me about you," she said.

"Whatever they said, they're lying."

"They say you like to fish." She said she could show him secret streams that had never before been fished by white men. Suddenly she reached out and he felt her fingers on the back of his neck. Her people were bark-peelers and her brown hands were rough from work. "Come," she said. "I taste like fish. I taste like the sea."

"Where?" He felt the tyranny of excitement.

"I know a place."

"What if your brother comes looking for you?"

"He'll be too drunk by now to go anywhere." Her dark eyes looking at him were full of light.

It was Jane Whitecloud who first took him into Temple Woods—"a place of God," she called it.

As soon as they entered Temple Woods, he felt languid, drowsy. He did not want to think about what he was doing. They came to a grassy bank and he laid down her mackinaw blanket and they sat there with their boots off.

"I bet you've got lots of girls in Portage," she said.

"Hardly any at all."

"I bet you've got a pretty girl at home, all right. Do you think she might lend you to me some nights?"

"I don't think she'd mind *too* much."

Then she was unbuttoning her red plaid shirt to reveal herself to him. She was no ordinary girl. Her body was slim, smooth, beautiful as something carved from wood or shaped from clay. His eyes explored from her breasts to the patch of black hair at the root of her belly. Her upper arms bore scars from the ritual triple cuts, and there was the tattoo of a jaguar on her shoulder.

It was the first time he had ever reached out and touched a beautiful body. She lay on the blanket. The sunlight streaming through the trees lit up her naked body. Fred felt his hands on her breasts. He felt the excitement stirring in his insides. She was like a deer suddenly moving to skittish life in the trees, the sudden leap of unsuspected life that brings the hunter's heart alive.

He feared he might explode as soon as he was inside her. Once he had buried himself inside her, he could not leave the place. Fred wanted to fill her up and stay there inside her, snug and tight. He felt himself sinking down in the lake, he was caught on the hook between her legs, she was dragging him down. He tried to jerk out, but each time some mysterious power drew him urgently back in again. It was all over in a few minutes. Immediately, he felt guilty. He stood and began to dress, looking down at the creature where his semen lay.

"Stay with me. You cannot go away from me now," she said. "I'll scream. My brother will hear me."

"No. He'll beat you. He'll think you're keeping the money."

"I don't go with men for money. I am not like Jenny Four-Fingers."

"I'm sorry. I didn't mean anything."

Nevertheless, he wondered if he had made a mistake not to have met the girl's brother first, in order to agree on a price and clear the air so the matter could be quickly forgotten.

But Fred could not forget this girl with skin the color of a deer. They met the next afternoon in the same place. He was already inside her, butting away, performing his urgent act. All he could think of was her, now.

He let her put her hand between his legs and stroke him, all her fingers gliding along the hard ridge, until he felt the insides of himself softening, getting ready to flow, her fingers probing. He retreated to a place of deep shade, so dark, so easeful that he felt his own face, his own thoughts go dark; then there was the eruption of light.

"Are you happy when we're together like this?" she asked him.

"Happy? No. It's different from happy." Then he was serious. "What will become of us?"

"What do you mean? Nothing will become of us. Why do you expect anything to become of us?"

She wrapped the blanket around her body.

He waited for her at the meeting place, the tall pine at the edge of the lake, the Wazee tree she called it, into which he had carved his promise, *Semper*, the word she had not understood until he had explained it was Latin.

She appeared in the smoky evening light, smiling at him. He felt his hands take off her shirt. He stripped the silent girl and immediately buried himself in her. The lake water lapped at her thighs. She spoke to him in her dark, beautiful language.

Her face showed her pleasure when he was inside her. They made love wherever they were able to—in the woods behind her brother's cabin; in the clearing among the aspens, where only the moon could look down and see them frolicking. He thought that he might die from exhaustion on top of her. But he was always pressing himself against her again, aching to enter her.

Sometimes they would go to the barn at one of the neighboring farms. They woke in the dawn light to the smell of manure, the cows looking at them, as though puzzled. Fred and Jane hurriedly dressed and left, before the milk maids should come and discover them.

It took Tom Whitecloud quite a while to understand why his sister was disappearing every night.

His father was still busy with the conveyancing of land titles and surveying the forests he was buying, millions of board feet of virgin white pine. The owners had tried to prolong the negotiations beyond reasonable limits, but there was no sign in his face of any strain from his business dealings.

Back at the inn, eating dinner and listening to his father talk about the land speculation, Fred felt almost himself again, sturdy, balanced, in right relations to the world. Then when he was alone in his attic room, the secret world of Jane grew further inside him.

He saw her shape again on the shingle roof and heard the familiar knock at the window. Sometimes they lay together until dawn, before she climbed out the window and crept back to her brother's cabin in the woods. And when Fred's father looked in an hour later to wake him for breakfast, he would remark that Fred looked utterly exhausted. Tired though he was, Fred could not sleep in the mornings, tormented by the feelings that raged through him for Jane. His heart thumped and he gasped for breath. It was like being ill.

His father was surprised by the seriousness with which young Fred undertook his fly-fishing now. Every morning Fred set off around the lake shore alone, with his fly-rod case and his rucksack. Nor did he show any sign of wanting his father's company. Fred seemed to want the solitude as much as the fish. His father thought that when his business was at an end he might cast a few flies himself, in order to discover the spot his son returned to every day so religiously.

Then one evening when he was lying on his bed, Fred was surprised by a knock at his door. It was his father, with a serious look on his face.

"Do you know what it means to be good?" his father asked him.

"Yes, Papa."

His father stopped him. "No," he said. "It seems that you don't know. Well, then I'll tell you. It means, what's good for helping us to love God, and God to love us. Do you understand that, Fred?"

"Father, I think I might go to sleep now, if you have no objection."

"We are many selves, not one. We are all of us sometimes surprised, or ashamed by our thoughts. Our thoughts are like voices in our heads. But we must not let our thoughts control us. We may not be able to control our thoughts. But our thoughts are not our deeds. You remember that."

"I'll remember, Papa."

"I can see you've got into this thing pretty deeply, Fred."

But his son turned his face to the wall; he had nothing further to say.

The next morning he was tardy in appearing for breakfast, and he felt his father scrutinizing his face.

"Reading too late last night, Fred?" he asked gently. "Better get more sleep. Don't want to arrive home looking like that. Don't want to worry your mother."

"I feel fine."

"We'll give the Indian village a rest today, I think," said his father. "I've still got four thousand acres of forest to see. I think you'd better come along with me. I might need some help."

They took the hired buggy down the logging road, past the primitive timber camp. It looked deserted. The men were away at work in the woods. Occasionally, somewhere in all that vastness, came the sound of an axe striking wood.

At noon, the two Indian girls came along the trail, carrying the bark-peelers' lunch pails. His father smiled at them and said, "Happy hunting."

The afternoon in the forest had grown dark. Jane knelt before him on the blanket and ministered to him with her mouth. And as she performed that act with him, he felt something of himself pass through his body and into her mouth.

From his first moment of communion with her, he had been aware of another presence on the forest floor, a spirit of immense power and authority. He was a magician, Jane said, one who could speak with the dead, the Manitouiriniou, she had called him, the Wonderful Man. He had come from far away, from another country, from Europe she thought it was. Her grandfather's grandfather's grandfather had seen him paddle into Green Bay near the site of the ancestral village, wearing a damask robe and carrying thunder pistols in both hands. He had called himself Jean Nicolet. Fred realized he had now entered an astonishing way of seeing. But it would not be until fifteen years later that he recognized the foggy shapes on the surface of the air in the glass photographic plates of Charles Van Schaick.

When he looked down at her it felt like when he was in the woods with his rifle in the still, early mornings, when he saw the sudden leap of color through the trees, and he felt his heart beating fast and the blood come tight into his face. He put the bullet in the breech, aimed it and, when he was about to fire, he felt the presence of a power greater than himself already ahead of him in the clearing, already standing over the deer, one who held the signature of death in the sinew of his strong shoulders and his bare brown arms. It was this spirit, who Jane had called the Manitouiriniou, who prefigured everything in the forest, who had already brought the deer down, hours before.

Now as Fred struggled on top of the girl on the soft pine-needle mulch, he also stood over the deer, which was kicking to die. Whatever was it she was staring at in the trees, that filled her eyes with such wonder? He remained silent, not wanting to disturb her reverie. Then Jane Whitecloud came back from wherever it was she had been and looked at him.

He had already had her a dozen times. Yet he felt the need to press into her in this urgent, final way. Fred did not understand exactly how it had happened on the forest floor that afternoon. He felt her relax, and she surrendered herself to him. She pointed her spine at his heart. But instead of pleasure, he had filled her with hot wounding pain. He felt the needle of pleasure plunge in and the tide of calm syrup flow through his limbs. And then, as Jane Whitecloud lay on her back in the woods, she opened the other mouth between her legs and gave birth to all that was stored in the memory of her tribe.

How was Fred to understand it, an Indian girl in the forest, her legs parted to give birth to these savage dreams? He was fifteen, of good family. He had never known bad women, wild women. Yet here he was in a secret place inhabited by overwhelming urges, and her voice hot in his ear telling him, "This is a thing that will last all of your life. You will never forget this way of seeing. I swear that from this day forth, wherever you are, I'll be there too."

Her glossy black hair faded in that moment and her face at fifteen was already old, as old as the oldest woman in her tribe. And at that moment Fred could see in her face the traces of what his own destiny would be. This place where they lay was already locked inside him. This was the same place where he would stand one day and Pauline L'Allemand would say, "Well, now she's gone and there's nothing you can do to bring her back."

He felt the veil of nausea fall through him. He did not understand the need in his hunter's heart to hurt her like this. Nor did he suspect then that he would return to that moment in the forest time and again, returning into her body until the end of his long life; then finally, as if into a grave.

Then Fred heard the noise. He looked across and saw

that Jane too had suddenly felt the presence in the trees. There was a parting through the goldenrod rushes, moving slowly in the breeze. The ground was not trampled, but the way the reeds swayed in the air gave him the feeling that someone had just passed by that way, something spectral, like a breath.

Fred had waited for her in the trees. Something was wrong. The sound of arguing voices came from inside the cabin. The faint voices faded away into the conspiring forest. Then Tom Whitecloud hit her once, the clean sound of an axe splitting a slab of wood. Then, because he was still mad and hitting her hadn't made him feel relieved, he hit her again. Fred had heard distinctly the sound of the blows, sharp slaps as clean as rifle shots. Then everything had gone very quiet in the cabin in the woods.

After the excitement, Fred suddenly felt very tired. For a long time he simply sat there, unable to do anything at all. Then he picked up his trout rod and set off alone to Temple Woods.

Each morning when he woke he told himself that he would not go back into the woods that day. He would resist the power of temptation. But three months of meeting her daily in the forest had their effect and he felt the hook drawing him back to Temple Woods.

But that afternoon he could tell right away there was something different about Jane Whitecloud. She was less sure of herself. Her eyes avoided his. Then she told him.

His first feeling was hilarity, as though she were making a joke. He laughed, then when his laughter stopped, he was as silent as the trees. He could not tell exactly how long he had been standing there without saying anything. Then he repeated the word she had used. "Baby."

In that moment they became separate, their lives divided and their roads led off in different directions. When he had begun to say the word, he was still full of the feeling of hilarity, but by the time he had said it, he had entered quite a different world. He knew several things in that new moment. He knew that he could not trust himself any more. He knew that he could not trust in his feelings, or in his natural impulse to decency. His word was now untrustworthy. Every word, every step forward now required caution. He could feel the net of the future tighten inside his gut.

They were two separate minds, two realities now; not a question of race, but of sleeping and waking, life and death, drinking and thirst. The girl in the woods who had knelt before him with so little shame or hesitation, who had opened her legs to him and begged him to fill her—where was she now? This ordinary Indian girl before him seemed to be someone else entirely. And yet when he recalled her savage yelp of pleasure as he had forced himself all the way into her, the muscles of his mouth held hard with the effort: all the other part of life, the part that was the Fred Turner he had thought himself to be, humane, ambitious, noble, decent, the life that still seemed bathed in the sunshine of promise, had suddenly vanished. He reached out and placed his hand on her stomach. He wept to think that they had made a little soul in there. It was as difficult a problem as could be for a young man. He loved her, but he hated her too, or he hated the part of himself that loved her. And very nearly at the same time.

He said, "The truth is, I cannot even begin to think of marriage."

He could see her teeth, feel her warm breath when she brought her mouth close to his face and said, "You may go away tomorrow. But you will always come back here."

His father was indulgent. "Don't you think it's high time we were getting you back home to school?" he asked, his eyes crinkled and kindly. His attention had been drawn to the matter by one of his associates. As his business was at an end there anyway, he would forgo the rest of the time he had intended to spend fishing, and they would return by the next train to Portage.

The next morning, Fred woke up to the reality of his having lost his innocence. He did not yet understand that whenever he was with a woman he would return to that first place, where he had entered Jane Whitecloud on the blanket in the darkness of the woods with the geese honking overhead, the fleeting figure disappearing down the trail, body dark as tanned hides, face pale with clay, the sound of water somewhere. Nor would he really understand for the next fifteen years why he returned to Balsam Point every summer.

The Turners, father and son, prepared to leave Balsam Point. Fred was already dressed, his suitcase packed, sitting on the side of his bed with a stunned look on his face. He was ashamed of his cowardice. Why were they leaving, anyway? Surely she would not come to the inn and confront his poor father? So. In time she would give birth. That's all there was to it. What did she want him to do? Marry an Indian girl? And yet, they had promised themselves to each other with such solemnity. He thought of himself carving *Semper* into the Wazee pine. Now he shuddered at what he had done.

The wood-burning steamer pulled away from the dock with a shriek upon its steam whistle and at that moment it sounded as Jane had the previous afternoon when he had taken her into the woods, the sound of Jane screaming.

11

FREDERICK JACKSON TURNER

"A dead girl in the ice shed?"

Turner looked hard at Robertson. The other man smiled the smile of one who knows something. From his hearty complexion and the way he stood with his elbow on the bar, he might have just cracked a good joke, and not just announced to someone the death of an innocent young girl.

"It's not Twyla, unfortunately. It's one of the milk maids from the farm down the road, Emma Tenn, a Swiss girl from Menominee. Head smashed in with a snow shovel. The farmer has made a formal identification." Then he added, "I say *unfortunately* only out of self-interest, you understand."

"It happened today?"

Now Robertson's expression changed. He grew serious,

thoughtful; the man of intelligence who was hiding beneath the bluff exterior now made his appearance. "It must have happened this morning. The farm supplies the inn here with milk, and it was one of the girl's chores to carry the milk pail up here to the ice shed after morning milking. The only thing is—we'll have to leave her in there. Does that bother you? You probably wouldn't want to eat those trout in there now anyway. A day or two. A week at the most. There will have to be an autopsy. The ice and frozen fish we've packed around her will preserve her. If the body is removed from the ice shed the processes of putrefaction will begin. Doc Krohn might take a few days to get here, with all the diphtheria. From the way her clothes are torn, it looks like the killer tried to rape the unfortunate girl, perhaps when she was already dead. Either he was interrupted, or there is some other explanation, but he didn't penetrate her to the extent of rupturing the hymen, according to the womenfolk." Robertson went on, "Yes, I am mystified. Unless you can supply an answer to my questions?"

"I'm as mystified as you are."

"Yes, of course you are. That is only to be expected. But you have been in that ice shed every day, have you not? Or is it that you have not been having such good luck with your fishing here this year? Could it be that for the last five days you have not caught any fish at all?"

"My fishing has borne me mixed results, that's true."

"But you did see this Swiss girl, Emma Tenn, at the ice shed this morning before you left for—wherever it is you go?"

"I did see a girl, yes. But I do not know whether or not

she was your Emma Tenn. She was carrying the milk pail. I've often seen her in the mornings."

"You go to the ice shed in the mornings to fetch your bait?"

"My bait? You're quite wrong there. You forget, Mr. Robertson, that I am strictly a dry-fly fisherman."

"Then why is it you did go to the ice shed this morning, Mr. Turner?"

"Yesterday afternoon when I came home, I left my trout rod there."

"So. You rose early to go trout fishing this morning. You went to the ice shed and saw the milk maid there, Emma Tenn with her pails. You made indecent advances to her, which she rejected. When she began to scream you put your hand over her mouth. You looked. There was no one else around, no one to witness your infamy. You dragged her into the ice shed and closed the heavy door. You ripped her clothes and tried to rape her. Then you picked up the snow shovel and smashed in her brains. Or did you try to rape her later? Maybe Doctor Krohn can tell us that. Well. You've heard my suggestion. What do you think about that?"

"I think your suggestion is vile."

"You reject it, then?"

"I reject it utterly."

"Good. I like a man who knows his mind."

"I have nothing to hide," said Turner.

"Nevertheless, I would very much like to search that little attic room of yours."

"Whatever for?"

"Blood traces on clothing, that sort of thing. Doc Krohn might want to have a look at that old Indian blanket of yours, for example. You have no objection, I take it?"

"As I said, I am not hiding any secrets."

"So. You are not hiding any secrets. You must be the only man in the world in that happy situation."

Turner's heart was racing from the aggression of Robertson's unprovoked attack on him. He felt the blood in his face and when he spoke the emotion in his voice was bare. "One thing, Robertson, before you go. It strikes me that you ought to have some evidence in writing that you are employed by the parents of this missing girl, Twyla Flake."

"Evidence in writing? Why no. I'm afraid you'll have to take my word for it."

"Or some formal identification from Pinkerton's."

"Formal identification," Robertson sniggered.

"The fact is that I should frankly be surprised if you work for Pinkerton's in Chicago at all. Now I come to think about it—you seem to know all the details about this poor girl so well, you could be the murderer yourself."

"Capital," Robertson was laughing his blustering laugh, hale and red in the face again. For a moment the oaf was back in charge of him. Then he said, "Actually, when the dogs went in yesterday, looking for Twyla, we did find something. There was a body in the woods, after all. Well, I should really say skeletal remains. Probably what the idiot boy saw and let his imagination get away with him. Been there for years. A young female by the looks of her. Who knows *what* happened to her? It's not Twyla, that's for certain. That's all that's of concern to me. It happened too long ago to be her. We don't even know who it is. My guess is it's

Memmie or Sadie or one of the others, though. And as for what happened to her?" Robertson spoke ironically now, as though he were quoting a line of poetry. "Time has stretched our knowledge to the bounds of conjecture."

"Perhaps it's a good thing," ventured Turner. "Let the poor creature rest in peace now."

"I'm afraid I can't agree with you there. You see, in my view, to simply leave it like that would bring her no peace at all. While her killer is free in the world. I confess, though, the way we treated that Billy Sunday boy reflects no credit on any of us."

Sheriff Buckley had concluded that the boy had been done a grave injustice, and that the brothers had a lot to answer for, taking the law into their own hands in that way. Jacob Rhinelander had claimed the skeletal remains Billy Sunday had found in the woods had turned out to be just an Indian girl who had gone off into the woods years and years ago and killed herself by taking strychnine. She had disappeared under the earth, and it was only after all these years that she had been laid bare again, the old shape pushing up from the dark world.

"Oh, by the way," Robertson turned back toward him. "I wonder if this would suffice?" He took something from his waistcoat pocket and offered it to Turner.

"I don't understand."

"You said you wanted identification of some kind."

Turner unfolded the piece of paper and examined it. It was an old account, stamped PAID, issued by the Pinkerton's Detective Agency, Chicago Office. Frank Murray, Superintendent. Robert Robertson, Assistant Superintendent. The bill, for forty-five dollars, had been made out to the

Ringling Brothers Circus, for services re: fakirs and pick-pockets. Telegraph, 18 words. 72 cents.

"Will that satisfy you? I used to work for the circus quite often, in the old days."

The door opened a crack. Pauline said in a wary voice, "We are not receiving visitors."

Turner told her that he needed to see Mr. Van Schaick on a matter of utmost urgency.

"That is impossible. Mr. Van Schaick is not here. There is only me and my poor Edgar. Mr. Van Schaick left here yesterday morning."

"Left here? How very convenient. What a remarkable coincidence." He explained to her what had happened to Emma Tenn in the ice shed the previous morning. "I'm sure that Sheriff Buckley will be interested to hear of this sudden departure."

"No. You don't understand. Mr. Van Schaick received a telegraph from his wife yesterday morning summoning him home to Black River Falls. Tragic news, I'm afraid. His infant daughter, Florence, has caught the black diphtheria and died." She seemed to relent, and the door opened a little more. "What is it you want?"

"Those photographs, the ones I looked at once before. The spirit photographs."

"The photographs? What about them?"

"I need to speak with you. About that—thing—that happened in the forest. People have been asking questions of me. I need your cooperation. To establish that what we saw that day was not—an ordinary girl." He might make

180

Robertson look at the spirit photographs. They were the only proof he had of what had happened. "Those spirit photographs. Are they still here, or did Van Schaick take them with him?"

Van Schaick had taken the glass plates, along with the rest of his photographic equipment, but he had left the prints with Pauline. "A girl in the ice shed?" Her face held hard; then, "Very well," she said. "I can see you are determined."

Pauline L'Allemand was obviously upset. Her skin had broken out in a rash. As she sat on the chair she scratched and rubbed the insides of her arms. The rash looked painful, as though something had rubbed her raw. Her nerves seemed strained. Edgar was nowhere to be seen. His little 20-gauge shotgun was propped on a chair beside the parlor window, with a line of cartridges. "We are very frightened," she explained. "Someone's been coming into our yard at night interfering with the chickens. Someone has even shot at our piano. I am convinced it is that savage, Billy Sunday."

The poor woman is at her wits' end, he thought. There must be *someone* persecuting her, to have got her into such a state. "But look here, a grave injustice has been done to that boy. The thing he found in the woods has been there for years. And now he's drowned in the lake."

Pauline said, "I wouldn't be so sure. You yourself said that a girl has been found dead in the ice shed behind the inn."

"It wasn't Twyla Flake, though," Turner said.

"Don't you see that Billy Sunday is responsible for that, too? I knew he'd come back here. He'll go on killing girls. I can sense him lurking in the trees out there, just waiting his chance to come into the house and kill us as well. Edgar has made me promise to keep all the doors and windows locked."

Even on her first day in the forest, Pauline said, she had felt the presence of the girl. She had climbed to the tower and stared in wonder at the vast wilderness which spread all around her. She felt there was someone in the darkness of the trees whom she already knew from sometime in the past. The forest seemed to be beckoning to her, to be drawing the very soul out of her. Even on that first afternoon she had heard the voice she had begun to suspect that in the stained mists of this forest there lingered some residue of evil.

The forest is our soul, the girl's voice said. *We will always be together here.* For days, Pauline had returned to the clearing to listen to the voice in the woods. She could not always understand what the voice was saying. It spoke sometimes in English but at other times the way the tongue fell on the teeth made her think she was hearing an Indian language, the way the Indians talk among each other. To hear the strange language was frightening—what else could it be but the Devil's language? She wondered if this girl's voice she was hearing in the woods could have had some message for someone in particular, who was in the immediate vicinity. She could see in his troubled eyes the story of his soul. Those strange words were trapped inside him, and Turner would need to have them exorcised, the way a child needed purging of its worms.

The story of his soul. Well. That was one way of putting it. Turner knew now that, however great the guilt and shame he felt, he would have to acknowledge that real love he had for so long denied. Only now did Turner begin to realize that he returned to Balsam Point each year to understand that order of savagery, sitting against his tree, waiting for the Indian girl to appear at the lake's edge.

Pauline fetched a pigskin case from the closet. She explained that it was a case she had taken with her to Dresden as a girl and in it she kept souvenirs from her life on the stage. The case also contained photographs of various circus artists, the acrobats and singers, the clowns and freak shows, the fakirs and necromancers. There must have been hundreds of the photographs.

There were also Van Schaick's photographs from that summer, the miserable creatures Turner himself had seen on his visit to the Indian camp. It was not only the filth and poverty, the faces ravaged by smallpox, but something in the pigmentation of their skin, tainted, iodine-colored, as though they had been cast out of God's gaze and sent naked back into the dark forest with its terrors and witches.

Turner's eyes leapt from image to image: a shape like a patch of snow on the ground; places he recognized close to the clearing by the lake shore; the Ringling Brothers Circus train, a woman's face carved into the band wagon.

Then he came to the face he had been expecting.

She was dressed in a feathered cloak, and wore moccasins of a striking zigzag design. Her eyes looked past the camera, past the man with his head under the black cloth. She stared at Turner as though she had suddenly remembered something, and all at once Turner realized where it was he had seen Billy Sunday's face before. It was like something he had known all along, and had had to make himself forget. Time telescoped, recognition sparked through the years and all at once Turner heard the creaking of wood, the heavy bump of the canoe landing on the lake shore, the steam whistle shriek of *The Lady of the Lake*, the sound of the paddlewheel like an arm beating the water.

In the photograph, Jane's face changed before his eyes. Her lips, now covered with sores, parted as though she would speak to him. She looked as though she had been baked in a slow oven. Her skin was shriveled and blackened, as though instead of through the natural processes of decomposition, the effects of air and water and time, it had been blackened in a fire.

But now it was Turner who was on fire. He felt the blood prickle hot in his face. His fists bunched into his temples, knuckles kneading his skull, trying to squeeze the painful knowledge back into Pauline and Van Schaick's insubstantial world of fog and mirrors, cameras and glass plates, knowledge without consequences. But *this* knowledge would not go away. In that maddening juncture between past and future when the needle of insight plunged in and the heat crept over his skin, Turner realized that Billy Sunday was his son, and there was light in the darkest vaults of his life and words in his deepest silences.

When Turner had returned with his father to Balsam Point two summers later, in 1879, everything had been different. He settled into his old room at the inn, the narrow bed with its mosquito net, the washstand with the hexagonal mirror, the same view over the shingle roof. Once again he occupied his days fishing and hunting. The best trout streams had been disturbed by loggers and blackened clearings scarred the landscape.

He did not see that companion of his youth. Jane Whitecloud had left Balsam Point. Someone said she had been seen working in a traveling circus. This information, casually gleaned, came as a relief to the young Turner. Nor did he see the Rhinelander brothers. All the boys had jobs in the timber camps now, and no one else spoke about her. Something had happened the previous year that no one wanted to talk about.

Then one day he had seen her in the woods. She hovered there in the clearing, wrapped in her owl-feather cloak, in the exact place where last time he had left her crouching on the grey blanket, her hindquarters exposed, wiping away his seed from inside her. His whole body clenched in terror. But when he finally found the courage to walk over and reach out for her, she vanished. All that was left of her was the smell of salmon rotting in the dry stream beds in the fall.

Pauline's superb voice had been wild with the promise of an impossible order, such as might have sprung up in the hearts of the old explorers, Marquette and Jolliet, those pilgrims into the bewitched world of the Algonquin and the Ojibwa, the Menominee and the Winnebago. But now, as she spoke, her whispering voice was like a horrible wind, taking him back to the nightmare of the forest, the dreams and desires of the moaning world he thought he had left behind. She spoke from the dead world, her face smudged with the charcoal light of the forest. The wind he heard was like the speech of the woods.

He was back in the trees again. The moss of time had grown over the bones of memory just as surely as it had covered the trunks of the pines and hemlock firs, but now as Pauline spoke, the sound of her voice cut through time. Her face changed as she spoke, became twitching and contorted again, the way it had looked that day in Temple Woods. The afternoon sun coming through the leaves outside the parlor window dappled her face with shadows, and he thought of stains in the mercury of an old mirror, spoiled photographic plates, shadowy shapes in the emulsion.

Jane Whitecloud had lain awake all night, listening to the crying from the woods. She knew that the voice of her lost baby was out there in the woods, but also still inside her, in the tight round shape of her belly where the little thing had once turned and kicked.

Her brother Tom had guessed about Jane's baby. It hurt Tom Whitecloud to bear witness to his sister's torment and madness. He saw her rise from her bunk in the night and follow the sound of the crying into the woods. He saw her disappear into the skeins of mist, wrapped in her mackinaw, and return at first light and silently crawl back into bed.

For days he agonized over what to do. Eventually Tom confronted her, and she confessed everything and explained how the baby was given up for adoption to the Wisconsin Benevolent Society.

Over the following nights, she continued to hear her baby's cries in the woods as though, wherever he was, whoever had him now was harming him, tormenting him. It was that which made Jane Whitecloud go into the woods and take the overdose of strychnine. From the porch of the inn at Balsam Point, they had heard her screams all night across the lake.

Now Turner looked at that dear, lost face. Jane had found no peace in death, but still heard her child's cries in the woods, and continued to search for him, restlessly. Turner had seen that pain in Billy Sunday's face, too, the way his eyes seemed hurt by the light of the world.

Only in the dreaming nights did she return to the site of their love. He heard someone moving in the dark in his attic room, feeling along the wall with her hands like a blind person. He called from his bed, "Who are you?"

"Open your eyes and see who I am."

The girl looked exactly as she had when he had first seen her, except that her face was white, miraculously bleached, and the dew of her soft brown eyes had turned to ice, glaucous, opaque. Since she had entered the solitude of death, her eyes had set. His hand shook as he reached out and touched her shoulder and upper arm. Her open sightless eyes stared up at him.

Turner was trembling. His head burned, and he felt the girl grow inward again, spread her tendrils through his blood. He reached out and touched the cold skin of her face, placed his hand over her mouth so that she would cry out for her lost baby no more. Her spirit might lie tormented forever among the ancient hemlocks, their trunks and branches limed with moss, the place where the dark branches met overhead and blotted out the sky, and hid her from the sky's gaze. She already had the surface of the bark in her. Her bones were tree. If only there was something he might do to give her peace.

Directly upon their return to Portage, young Fred had begun to display the symptoms of an illness. His mother gave him iron tonic to enrich his blood. She saw at once that her son had become another person. The difference between her son who had gone away to Balsam Point for the summer and the one who had come back was like twin brothers who grow apart in life and end up looking different to each other. "Don't worry, Mama," he said. But she was worried.

For several days all he wanted to do was sleep. She sent in a couple of the neighboring boys, his closest childhood friends, to cheer him up, but Fred's craving for sleep got the better of him. Then there were the headaches and fever. Whereas before all he could do was sleep, now he was tormented by an unnatural wakefulness. In the night time, in the dark, he heard her voice. He was trapped inside the sound of her voice. He suffered the fevers and excruciating headaches in silence, at first. After all, they were no more than he deserved. It wasn't until he screamed with the pain that the doctor was called in.

The doctor diagnosed an inflammation of the meninges. The officer from the State Board of Health was informed:

viral meningitis was mosquito-borne, and not at all un-common in the north woods where Fred had spent the summer.

By December, he was seriously ill. The pain arrived punctually, a man on a mule that turned its hindquarters toward him and kicked him repeatedly in the head. He felt the pain rage through him, until he stood again in the clear-ing in the forest, confronted by the Manitouiriniou, the face of clay.

All that time he spent in his sickbed, he was physically away from that most feared place. But in the pitiless fevers, he was back there again. The smells of the damp earth, veg-etation and feces spread all around him, contaminating him. The air turned a dark yellow, then brown, like the tones of a sepia photograph.

The possibility of death seemed so inviting. He scarcely noticed when his own mother came into the room. He was not even able to form his words properly. Just imagining Jane having his child and giving it up was enough to make him stop feeling, stop living. He could not bear to admit to himself that he had committed such an outrage. One day when he looked in his old rucksack and saw her shell bracelet in the bottom, he heard a horrible, choking voice say *"Semper"* and he dropped the bracelet in horror, like a murderer recoiling from the one piece of evidence that could hang him.

He could not even get up from bed with the headache. All he could see was the girl's open eyes glazed with ice. There won't be an end to this until I wind up in the mad-house, he thought.

By New Year's Eve, when he heard the pealing of the

church bells, he had reached the crossroads. "What a pity. A boy like him. He could have been the President, if he'd set his mind to it," he heard his father say, at the fireside.

"Don't talk of him as if he's gone." His mother feared for his life, and blamed her husband for taking the boy back to the north woods, to the lakes and swamps infested with mosquitoes.

The truth was that his poor mother was frightened even to go in and check on her son. She dreaded the smell of his illness. It was as though the very air in that room was stained with the contamination. The smell in there was awful, like rotting fish. She avoided passing by the churchyard on days when she knew a funeral was being held. Even so, she would unintentionally glance through the window of the carpenter's shop where pine coffins were built.

But his mother knew that he did sometimes get out of his bed. She could hear him moving about in there at night. She could hear fingernails scraping at the walls. Perhaps Fred was trying on his clothes to see how much weight he had lost? In her darkest moments, she suspected him of play-acting, from motives she could not even guess at. Now his friends did not visit him. He who had been the most popular of his class, whose opinions were sought out, who had been so influential, had faded to a shadow. When his fever sufficiently abated for him to dress and leave his sickbed, his lassitude and apathy continued. His mother often asked him gently, with love, "Now where's the Fred Turner I used to know?"

———

He had seemed completely cured, except when someone heard him cough, a painful bark that echoed through the gloomy interior of the general store. Or when, suddenly weak, he couldn't stand up anymore, and had to sit down wherever he was and rest. His indolence, an outward calm that surrounded this stage of his convalescence, hid the struggle in his soul. The boy still endured the visitations. Hallucinating in his fever, he had seen the closet door open. The actual girl invaded his room and walked toward his bed as if she had some particular business with him.

In the nights, he saw again the phantom girl, fleeing from him through the trees of the forest; seeking refuge in a last sacred place, where the bones of her grandfather and great-grandfather were buried, a mound of egglike rocks, marked with eyes and tears. A place whose sanctity she thought even a white boy could not be impious enough to violate. If only he could see what sacrilege it was.

In his fever, he crossed again the forest floor alone with the garden spade to their old place in Temple Woods, where he knew he would find her. The rain was loud in the trees. He could not bear to face a moment longer the thought of her being dead because of him. If he could bury her, he thought, it might give her spirit peace.

He had found what was left of her wrapped in her mackinaw in the hollow of an old hemlock's roots, not far from the tree she had called Wazee, where his word, *Semper*, had been carved. She had become one with the floor of the forest. Tender chanterelle mushrooms grew from her body. Wild dogs, or some other beast, had fed on her. Savage teeth had ripped away her clothing to get at her flesh; the meat of her thigh had been stripped to the bone.

The veil of nausea descended around him and he found it difficult to breathe. All the same, he wanted to be with her, to just sit quietly by her. He felt that she would be aware of his presence, somehow.

But her spirit would not be quiet. Jane Whitecloud returned to the world, rose up from that mossy hollow and beckoned to him, as though she desired to impart some urgent message to him. Perhaps she wanted to tell him what had become of their child, so that he might claim it as his own, and take care of it. He heard her speech in the trees, though now her words in the Winnebago language were unintelligible to him.

Her spirit rose up from the mossy earth and she was whole again. She opened the front of her red shirt for him, just as she had the first time. He took the tip of one of her breasts into his mouth, and he felt her push her wet mound against him as she had when she had been alive, and he moved into her again and rode her blindly, his face twisted, ugly, violent, his tears falling on her. He tried to bring her back to life. Her skin felt cold and reptilian; then the warm sap rising through his body killed memory, and he lost himself in her. Then, when he had bled himself into her and had withdrawn, he tried to lift her.

He sat as though in her lap, with her arms over his shoulders, then tried to stand and lift her that way. Then he tried to pull himself forward onto his knees. He tried to increase the pressure, but he was still unable to fit her in the place. He pulled with all his strength. The knuckles of a giant were pressing into his back. It was no use. He would have to drag her. He propped her against the trunk of the tree in her unsteady sitting position but she would not stay there. He broke her arms at the elbows to get them to sit the right way in that shallow grave he had dug for her between the roots of the tree. He heard the sinews in her arms pop. He buried her in the hollow earth made by the tree's great roots bulging up out of the earth.

He sat, not speaking, in his chair in his parents' sitting room in Portage, his blanket wrapped around his shoulders the way she used to wear hers, against the recurrence of the fever. He dreaded the onset of those chills so much, he was never without his blanket now. The boy had withdrawn more and more into his own cold silent world.

Not until the spring of 1881 was he well enough to return to college in Madison and resume his studies. A mask of normality covered his days, and normality was what he craved after all this time. He resolved to live with his secret, to hide it away until that event might be shrouded in time, until the glacier of forgetfulness should creep down and cover the contours of the remembered landscape. Balsam Point might be forgotten, at last.

But the more he had struggled to forget, the closer he was to the Wazee trail, and the sense of secret intention in the forest lived on in him, drawing him back there, like a moth to the flame. The life of that lost infant, and the mystery of what had become of it, continued to shape him.

Year after year, he made his "fishing trips," and returned to Temple Woods, an annual pilgrimage to that lonely place, the clearing in the forest. In his trances, when he returned and sat at the lake shore, staring out over the water, she returned to him, miraculously restored, pure, unstained, undefiled. They were alone together, and they enjoyed their victory over death. She was the only one he had ever wanted, the only one who could heal him, soothe away his fever, cure him of his terrible thirst.

12

BILLY SUNDAY

Billy Sunday plucked up the courage to take a ride on the new, giant steam-driven Ferris wheel that had recently been purchased by the circus and set up in Baraboo. He felt, when he was at the topmost point of the ride, that he had come to a dead stop in the revolution of the earth. Then, with each descent of the giant wheel, the earth swooped closer and he felt the wind roar past his face. Each time the ground sped by, he realized there was an intention behind this pattern of movement. The ground was waiting for him. He saw before him a sharply defined, broad bar of afternoon sunlight. In the column of light stood the figure of the Wonderful Man.

He felt the Holy Spirit enter him. There was a feeling of intense glowing heat in his abdomen, as if Fate had stretched its hand into his entrails and tugged upon a golden cord, straightening his course in life, pulling him from inside his own guts into the future, onto the true path of his destiny. He felt a sense of warmth and belonging, as if, somehow, he had just found his mother and father. It was at that moment precisely that there was a sudden jolt in the coupling of the swinging seat.

Until that moment, Billy Sunday had always thought that messages were a matter of words; but this message was a direct line of truth, wordless guiding light, and he knew he was in mortal danger. Far less than faith or certainty, he was filled with an alarming doubt. This transcendental communication could lead him equally to the madhouse as to the mansion of the heavenly Father. Was this really the experience of Jesus Christ, or was he being drawn instead away from the backwoods and the orphanage of the Wisconsin Benevolent Society and the timber camps and the Boarding House for the Young Poor and the photographer's dusty studio and into the Old Necromancer's trance, as into a net of evil?

Billy Sunday had been born with the shame of the Old Necromancer already contaminating his heart. So be it. It must have been God's will. Billy Sunday now resolved that he would strive hard to perform good works. He would uphold the faith, and help spread God's Word in order to wipe away that stain of sin from his heart.

Jim Whalen had just gone outside to enjoy his afternoon cigar, when he saw the coupling on the Ferris wheel snap and the seat soar through the air and the boy still in it, graceful as a bird. At first he had thought it was an angel he was seeing, because the flying boy was surrounded by a prism of light. Then the column of rainbow light through which the boy moved turned to smoke and vanished.

As Billy Sunday moved through the air, the bread of his belly swelled, he felt the sudden thud of the earth, and the cold feces passed through his bowels.

A howl broke from his body, a howl of fury for himself that he had been chosen, the rage of being awakened when he would just as rather have slept. He resented God for choosing *him* for His ministry. He would not now be able to hunt down the Old Necromancer and kill him. He felt the rage of God's love, a love that had arrived in a single moment, in a circus ride, with such force that it had hurled him through the air and onto the snowy ground, from where he had stood and walked off without injury.

Billy Sunday did not understand what he had just experienced. He had always thought one had to be in church or reading the Gospel to learn about Jesus. But these seeds had sprouted in the dark until this moment, when they had suddenly grown into a perfect tree. In the years he had been living in the timber camps, then when he had gone into the forest near Balsam Point, he had tried to penetrate that celestial canopy and failed. When he had gone into the forest and heard Pauline's voice singing to the lost souls, and had felt that terrible desire rip through his body, Billy Sunday had looked up to God for an explanation. When he remembered the low branch with the noose swaying, he understood now that those injustices at Balsam Point last summer had been a kind of preparation for this. But those stains that had been trying to reveal themselves to him in the photographic plates were part of his destiny, too. The thing that made the forest tremble, even when there was no wind.

The thing that gave speech to the voices when the trees creaked, the dark trees became the sky, the ceiling of the world. They were part of it, too. Not God. Something else.

The first day in Temple Woods, when Pauline had disrobed and stepped into Billy Sunday's mind. He remembered not her ample white flesh, but her voice as she sang. He had thought it so beautiful, it must have been the voice of God, but now he knew different. Temple Woods was a place of evil. The woman's voice that spoke to him in tongues. The sly way the words formed in his head. The Devil's tongue insinuating itself warm into his ear, telling him to do those terrible things. The way he had let his wet seed slide out of his body. After he had done it, he had been so scared he couldn't even say the evil one's name, and he knew now that the Old Necromancer had been near him.

Billy Sunday was standing on an orange crate, preaching to the little crowd that had gathered in the meeting house.

By now there were regular faces he recognized, mainly the tramps who went begging for food from farm to farm, and who more often saw the wrong end of a shotgun than a plate of bread and milk. Billy Sunday looked like a tramp himself, in his old black coat.

These vagrants were a growing problem for the authorities. Gangs of them rode into town on the roofs of trains. The tramps themselves were often armed, and assembled in the public parks and the railroad stations, demanding handouts and menacing passersby. It took policemen assisted by a number of citizens to run them out of town.

Outside Baraboo, a barn had burned down and a child

burned to death. "Incendiaries" were blamed and a group of destitute men rounded up from the riverbank where they had been camping, not far from the Ringling Brothers compound, and locked in the town jail. When they were released, they ended up in the meeting house, listening to the preacher. At least it was warm in there. Billy Sunday scanned their faces, looking for one in particular who might conceivably have been, sometime in the past, an itinerant mesmerist.

In his sermon, Billy Sunday criticized McCracken's Perpetual Motion Machine, a new addition to sideshow alley. He had watched the great pendulum of the Perpetual Motion Machine repeat its obsessive movements, swinging through the thirty-two points of the compass. It came to a complete rest at one point, then began its journey again. To Billy Sunday's mind there was something arrogant in this invention. Perpetual motion was something outside God's laws. What could it be but the Devil's device? Everything in this world must be subject to the laws of waning, the death and corruption of the flesh. Otherwise, how could there be promise of the Life Eternal? Billy Sunday had come, since last summer at Balsam Point, to think of the camera as a Devil's device, too. He had come to think of the camera's gaze as a form of hatred.

It was the weirdest feeling in the world to hear himself speaking. To be up there on the orange crate and looking down at all those hatted heads. To hear the words of the Gospel emerge fully formed from his mouth, effortless and perfect. All his years of reading the Bible had had their effect. Even at the height of his sermon, as he heard his own excited voice coming from somewhere else, and somehow the hallelujahs bursting from his throat, from the darkness that had not known it contained them, the other darkness of Temple Woods lived on. And however much the love of God might lift him up through the shafts of rainbow light, and give him the Old Necromancer's voice to spellbind his audiences, Billy Sunday knew that there was some meaning back there in those woods still waiting for him.

The other circus people would have nothing to do with him. They thought the boy who worked with the canvas handlers had gone plain crazy. The step from Billy the rope boy to Billy the preacher was too great for them to take. They would hiss sarcastic comments to each other when he passed by.

Billy Sunday was also the subject of jealous discussion among local clergymen. They complained of the growing number of people he attracted to his meetings at the winter quarters of the circus; and the fact that he looked Indian. He used another Indian, Peter Coyote, to assist him with things like chairs and collections. Peter Coyote had himself been a lay preacher, but his words were as nothing compared with the gift of Billy Sunday. The Reverend Donald A. Hunger came to his defense: "As long as we're all spreading the word of God, there can't be any harm to it." And if Billy Sunday did on rare occasions fall to the ground like an epileptic, speaking in tongues, what was that but the Holy Spirit? And if he claimed to be able to heal the sick and make whole the cripples—well, wasn't there a precedent for that set down in the Bible, too?

Billy Sunday walked humbly into the meeting hall and stood in his black coat and starched collar. It was a clear winter night outside, and the blue-black blanket of the sky was impregnated with stars. A sprinkling of fresh snow lay on the roofs of the houses. While the ladies chattered in their seats to conceal their nervousness, their menfolk congregated in the far corners of the room, conversing with each other with exaggerated enthusiasm. Of all the men in the room, only Billy Sunday stood apart, refusing to socialize in any way.

At the beginning of his sermon, it was the severity of his expression that made the biggest impression. His language was simple, biblical, not at all learned. His lips seemed effortlessly to form the words in the everyday language already written in their hearts. He talked of corn and barn fires, of "birling," the way he had first seen men walk on water when he was twelve, crossing the river log to log. He talked of God in the same way as easy evenings in the yard, with the comforting bump of dishes in the wash pan inside and the yelps of the little ones playing. He spoke of God in the woods, of His mystery enacted in the simple acts of hunting and fishing; for the God he talked about was a midwesterner. Billy Sunday's homespun, uneducated preaching struck a chord with his audiences of plain rural folk, not yet even a generation removed from the frontier experience.

Sometimes when he was already preaching, Billy Sunday felt another voice entirely rise inside him. He heard that mesmerizing voice ring its heroic rise and fall around the walls of that simple meeting house in Baraboo, the winter quarters of the Ringling Brothers Circus. His religious mania seemed out of place in one still so young.

Bertha Thadeus, one of the prostitutes who followed the circus, was used to harsh treatment. She knew and feared the men who had her, who came out of the timber camps on a Saturday night, drunk, yelling at the tops of their voices in their strange Nordic languages, hungry for a woman. They didn't care what they did to her. There was no tenderness in them, they hated themselves and her too for what they were doing. They spurted inside her then slapped her around, broke furniture and smashed the windows. So she did not mind when Billy Sunday paid his furtive visits.

Beyond the bed, the sounds of the night came to him. Snatches of song from a group of carousers. A shout, sudden as a gunshot. The screech of an elephant. The growls of caged beasts, snarling, nocturnal. At these times, there was no eloquence in Billy Sunday, none of the oratory which flowed so easily from his tongue when he was before an audience. He seemed bereft of language, the way a man who was dead drunk was beyond language, the way Indians spoke little, using speech only when it was necessary, preferring signs and gesture. They existed in a supernatural world beyond language.

And it was when Billy Sunday was silent like this, lost in a place beyond words, when he watched her with his beast's eyes, small and pinched with pain, but as cold and emotionless as an elephant's or a head upon a totem, she came to feel afraid of him. It was as though there was an older man in his body, the wild old man who leapt into Billy Sunday and showed in his eyes when he preached. So that when Billy Sunday visited her, she saw the other man in his eyes, and was afraid, and tensed up when his hard little fingers came too close to her throat in the bed.

Billy Sunday's reputation spread beyond the confines of the circus and soon people from outlying farms and even from as far away as Portage were journeying to Baraboo for his Saturday afternoon prayer meetings. This young preacher from the backwoods was a marvel. He was so unlikely a candidate to wear the charismatic mantle that his celebrity spread all the more quickly. His wooden face seemed more refined when he preached. There was a quick, feminine intelligence in it.

These Revival meetings, now held in one of the big empty barns with red-painted corrugated iron walls, sometimes lasted for hours. Everyone was talking about the circus boy with his message of personal salvation through Christ. But there was a limit to how far people could travel in a Saturday to hear him, and Billy Sunday began to think about casting his net further afield.

Although his voice began low and humble, the voice of one who had known torment in his life, he was a member of a circus (even if he was only a rope boy and canvas handler) and he had learned that one eats by one's performance. He began collecting money for his Revival. People were pleased to give a dollar, sometimes more. After that first collection, Billy Sunday's old leather satchel contained nearly fifty dollars.

He spoke without pause through snowstorms, through howling winds. Billy Sunday began in a low voice which gradually got louder, and the audience felt the floor and walls tremble around them, as though one of the elephants was moving around. His flights of language retraced his own flight through the air, the moment he had seen the prism of light and had personally come to know the experience of the Wonderful Man.

His preaching was different from any they had ever heard, more gentle, more homely. Whereas his audience was well acquainted from other preachers with the geography of Hell, the eternal flames, the bottomless pit, the blood-sweating Behemoth, Billy Sunday's sermons led them into a different terrain, the virgin pine forests that stretched all around them. He had the gift of making Hell a personal place, in the north woods, close to home. He led them into the Hell of the forest so dark and deep, that when they came back from their trance they looked at each other with strange eyes. They might have just awakened from a long sleep, they looked so bewildered. And they reached out and touched a neighbor's shoulder, the back of the neck of the person sitting in front. And that was the moment when Billy Sunday fell silent, and knew enough to remain silent.

The first sound came from a throat in the audience, a lonely bleat, like a question, and straight away the bleats of the others answered him. The first had been an incoherent sound, but as it was joined by the others it grew into full hallelujahs.

All the time, Billy Sunday continued to work hard for Jim Whalen, Superintendent of Canvas. Star performers of the circus felt they were being overshadowed by a mere rope handler, and Billy Sunday's preaching was often the subject of their jokes. Billy Sunday paid no heed.

Then the days of darkness were upon him again. These periods of headaches and depression were like stains upon his sight. From his sickbed, it felt that nothing would ever lift his dark weight of sorrow. He often wondered about the stains he had seen on Van Schaick's glass plates. And all the time now, the story of the Old Necromancer and Lalla Rookh continued to eat like a stain into his fate.

Lying in his bed, Billy Sunday sometimes felt he was running backward through time. Sixteen years earlier, a man had milked himself into the body of a sleeping woman and that was the beginning of everything that had followed. He imagined Lalla Rookh, lying like a sleeping princess on the Old Necromancer's bed, covered with his damask cloak.

Billy Sunday wondered about the grave that had been dug for him. He often recalled the way Edgar had said, "Oh hell, Billy Sunday. Why did you ever have to go and find her?" There were times when Billy Sunday relived his journey through the water, and that strange creature he had found under it, Twyla Flake belted to the cider press, wondered how she had met her end, what order of existence had swallowed her up. She was newly dead, the day before, perhaps. Her open eyes were still full of the wonder of the light that had enveloped her, and her floating hair explored the wobbly aqueous light restlessly, as though desiring something.

When he was sitting at the table with his Bible in the evenings, his fingers kneading his temples from the headache, he would suddenly see that astonished face again and his heart pounded inside his chest so loud he leapt up from his chair as though he had been bitten by something. "What is it?" Bertha Thadeus asked, startled. He sat down again, not wanting to call attention to what tormented him.

Then at two in the morning he would see her face again, and come soaring out of sleep into the bricks and mortar of the wakeful world. Still the open eyes and streaming hair pursued him from the realm of sleep. She might have been an angel bathed in that watery light, except the leather belt marrying her to the cider press bit into her flesh in such a mortal way.

He knew that he might still be a wanted man in Balsam Point. It was unlikely, however, that word would find its way to the north woods, or even into the *Badger State Banner* in Black River Falls, about the exciting new revivalist, Billy Sunday, in Baraboo. Mr. Van Schaick might never discover what had really become of his former apprentice. It was unlikely anyone would make a connection between this charismatic preacher and the boy who had been a photographer's apprentice in another part of the state the year before and had disappeared in the lake.

So there was no reason for Billy Sunday to feel hunted anymore. But the thing was he did still feel like that. A shadowy fate was pursuing him, running him to ground.

Billy Sunday had been marked out by the Lord in this way. He belonged to a secret brotherhood of those who had been inducted into the freemasonry of the woods. And, feeling this, his eyes were again those of the destitute fourteen-year-old who had limped into Black River Falls and saw the sign PHOTOGRAPHIC GALLERY, his eyes full of pain, his face as mute as wood.

Now, in 1893, with the Depression, the banks closing, the bankruptcies and suicides, the increasing number of cases of madness, the killing of tramps and burning of barns, he saw the same fear in other people's eyes.

One night a woman came to Billy Sunday's candlelight prayer meeting in the big barn at Baraboo. She had walked for miles to get there through the slanting sunlit landscape under the dark thundery sky. She had the look of poverty upon her, her dark clothes unwashed, a streak of dirt on her cheek, like ashes. She sat in the congregation in Billy Sunday's barn. It later turned out that she was De Witt Edwards's wife, and on her return home she killed herself and their ten-year-old by placing arsenic in their cups of chocolate.

The economic crisis of 1893 was in many ways a turning point in American history. The feeling that something had gone terribly wrong in the system destroyed people's confidence. On August 24, 1893, the Bank of Black River Falls, capital $10,000, failed and shut its doors. Someone tried to shoot O'Hearn, the bank treasurer. There were many bank failures, those years.

Billy Sunday heard about cases of hardship from the people who asked for his help. Other cases he read about in the *Baraboo Times*, the *Wisconsin State Journal* and the *Badger*

State Banner. Tramps stole into a farm and beheaded eighteen chickens. John Ovenbeck of Friendship, Winnebago County, refused food to tramps. The tramps entered his barn and cut the throats of three cows, which bled to death. They left him a note, explaining their actions. Mrs. Tobias, a recent widow, was convinced that someone was coming in the house at night. She complained to Mr. and Mrs. Bailey, who owned the house in which she boarded, about these intrusions in the night, something disturbing the horses and chickens. Then there came the night when the baby was gone. Mrs. Tobias headed straight to the stables, where she found, according to the *Badger State Banner*, the horse eating her baby.

Curtis Ricks, the "bone man," whose skin had begun to ossify eight years before and who had been working for the past two years in the Ringling Brothers Circus, died. General Olson was charged with the incest of his stepdaughters aged eleven and twelve. William McCarty, the wild man of Spaulding's Lake, was captured and taken to the Mendota State Hospital. Poitr Romanovich, the hermit of Temple Woods, was declared violently insane by doctors and taken to Mendota. Mamie Weeks, of Beaver, made a complaint against her father, Jacob Weeks, as the father of her unborn baby.

Mary Ricks, the "Wisconsin Window Smasher," was arrested for the hundredth time and put into jail. Mrs. Ames of Rock County, left by her husband in their cabin without fuel or food, froze to death. Her baby was found buried under the snow in a soap box. Thomas Galt died from the effects of the Ackerman Anti-Dipsomania Gold Cure. Clifford Bell, a colored attaché of a traveling show, was ar-

rested at Plainfield and taken to Mauston. He was charged
with the abduction of a pretty Mauston girl.

The diphtheria epidemic showed no sign of abating.
There was a large number of deaths. Schools were closed,
and whole communities put under quarantine. It was common to see policemen stationed outside to guard the houses
where the infection was present. The disease affects the
membrane in the throat and makes breathing difficult.
Children were particularly vulnerable. Andrew Hoffman
of Oshkosh had four children die of diphtheria in five
weeks. Henry Miller of Cedarburg had five children die in
a month. The grim situation was summed up in the *Badger
State Banner* in the November of that year: "The epidemic
has given such alarm that it is hard to induce the living to
bury the dead."

Billy Sunday had come along at the right time. Most people, over the next three terrible years, had friends or neighbors who had gone mad, killed all their cows for no reason,
set fire to their crops, burned down their farmhouse or
barn. As a lay preacher, whose fame was growing by the
day, Billy Sunday was allowed to follow private paths into
their desolate lives. He was accepted into strangers' houses
by suffering people, where, as soon as he had stepped under
the lintel, he felt the house, or something in it, rebel against
his presence. He heard the walls ticking, the house frame
twisting, the door frames warping out of alignment.

And it was at times like these that Billy Sunday would
show up, not so much to help the deranged, as they were already gone to jail or to the State Hospital at Mendota, as to
comfort those who were left behind, poking a boot toe
through the rubble and ashes where their home had been,

shocked, uncomprehending faces among the images of devastation and abandonment. And Billy Sunday would tell them simply that he had been an abandoned child too. With God's help they would have a home again, and prosper.

He was also called upon to comfort the bereaved. Even the most terrible sights did not arouse pity in him. Maybe that explained his phenomenal success as a preacher: people mistook his fierce belief at eighteen for wisdom.

He found one woman kneeling at the beside of her dead husband. In that house, shuttered and airless, the light seemed brown, stained with death. He heard the charlatan's voice begin inside him, independent of himself. "A person does not die when he stops breathing, when the heart stops beating and the flesh goes cold," the voice began. A rush of heat filled his face, and he felt a sudden stirring, like a gust of wind filling a dead flag. "The body dies, but it is the body only. We bury the body, but we can dig it up again and see its corruption. The life which is the body here can be counted in days. But the life everlasting cannot be counted in days or weeks or even years. It cannot be buried, or dug up, because it is incorruptible."

Sometimes a member of the public sent him a message asking him to attend with prayers in their house if someone was sick. One Tuesday a mother whose child was suffering from the black diphtheria sent word to Billy Sunday in Baraboo, imploring him to come and attend to her.

When he arrived, the woman, the wife of a poor farmer, fell to her knees and begged Billy Sunday. She could not bear to see her child die, she said. She had already buried three. Her Becky was the only one she had left. The mother's anguish was pathetic to see. She wept, begging him to use his faculty as the prophet of God's love. Yet at that moment all he felt was a hardness of heart.

Billy Sunday stood in silence, in his dark clothes, his starched collar fastened with a stud at his throat. He was usually gentle and tender in his speech with women, but now he spoke with pitiless clarity, as though he were delivering one of his Saturday afternoon speeches and the older, other voice came out of him. He told her that everyone always asked the question about how an innocent little child or even a little baby getting sick and suffering and dying could be an expression of God's will, much less of His love. Well, Billy Sunday believed he had an answer to that.

It was only at the end that we invoke God's help in quite that way. It was the thought of dying that brought the Lord's name to our lips. He shows us by His Word and His actions that His love is invincible, that no dark power in Hell can destroy His love for us. These tribulations in the fleshy world come, not exactly as a test of our faith, but the more terrible the thing to happen to us, shows just how great His love for us is.

We must accept our tribulations, exalting in His love, even those who had been tardy to respect Him before. We must respect Him blindly, for He is our Lord and Superintendent. So that hearing His name exalted by the sinners and the tardy, He might take a loved one from them, so that they might understand that they must love God absolutely, and subject themselves to His will without questioning, no matter how bad the thing that might happen. This was the only way for her to understand the blissful experience of absolute faith, the sublime feeling of being one of the Lord's children, of belonging, of having family.

Billy Sunday said that we catch the black diphtheria and other contagion from the blood of strangers, that all of us are sons of the Fallen Angel, true inheritors of his gifts and seed. And when one of us sins in his heart, it spreads a black stain in the world through us all. This was the meaning of contagion. Her little girl Rebecca might yet live, and grow up, and marry and bear children, just like Rebecca of old in the Book of Genesis, wife of Isaac, mother of Esau and Jacob: "And the Lord said unto her, Two nations are in thy womb, and two manner of people shall be separated from thy bowels; and the one people shall be stronger than the other people; and the elder shall serve the younger."

As he spoke, he became aware that the mother was moving. Her physical presence was alive with moving shadows. The air in the room had gone darker, suddenly thick with brown cobwebs. Billy Sunday felt the shadow of the cobwebs close over his face, he stumbled against the edge of the table, upsetting the inkwell which had been left there after she had written her message to him. He felt the darkness would have its final victory over him this time. Then he saw the column of golden light enter the room and suffuse the brown dust like a halo of sunshine.

The column of light measured a yard across, but it was growing faster all the time with a sound like the wind, like an accordion slowly expanding. Billy Sunday realized that the child's soul was leaving the house. He saw from the astonished look on the mother's face that she had seen the light, too, and he clenched his fist into his temple, like he had one of his headaches, or as though by an effort of will he would draw that golden light back into the house.

212

The woman rushed into the bedroom to find the child dead in her cot.

Peter Coyote had been converted by Baptist missionaries in the north woods, but his real conversion had come when he had seen a spirit standing in a shaft of smoky light in the middle of the trail one day in the forest. Peter Coyote had stopped dead, as if a snake had crossed his path. His stillness stretched back in time to the greater stillness of the forest before his birth, before the first white man had disturbed it. Peter Coyote, a poor bark-peeler in his cavalry trousers, wearing his frayed blanket, confronted the spirit hovering just ahead of him in an aura of golden smoke.

At first, Peter Coyote thought it was his great-grandfather, a guardian spirit who appeared to him from time to time in the form of a leopard, a mythical animal in these north woods, especially when he was hunting deer. He did not know whether his great-grandfather spirit appeared to him to warn him of danger, of the proximity of deer; or simply because, in the last century, his great-grandfather had enjoyed hunting so much.

Peter Coyote's people had been taken from their lands of woods and stream and lake and herded into railroad cars by Federal troops and taken to a reservation in Nebraska. The emptiness of the plains was terrifying to the Winnebagos, who were unused to hunting in the open. Besides, they were far from where their own guardian spirits lived. They had no ancestors in Nebraska to direct them to food. This was Sioux land. Many of them had simply started walking, and within a year they were back in Wisconsin.

During the previous decade, the Ghost Dance religion, arising from the dream revelations of Wovoka, had begun to be practiced. The new teaching had reached his people in 1889, and took the form of a prophecy of a deliverer who would restore the Indian race, living and dead, to a regenerated earth, the green world as it had been when the white explorers had first laid eyes on it.

For the past few years, the government had been trying to stamp out the Ghost Dance, especially among the rebellious Sioux. Sitting Bull had been killed on December 15, 1890, and, two weeks later, at Wounded Knee, more than two hundred men, women and children had been massacred by troops.

There was no rebellion in Peter Coyote's own people anymore. They had been tamed, just like the animals in the circus. His people had lost their living animal hearts. But they still continued the ceremony of the Ghost Dance, believed to bring the dancers into communion with the souls of dead friends.

Now, here was the spirit appearing to him, baptising him back into a brotherhood of leather and wood that went back much longer than the Jesus-on-the-cross. He knew it was the guardian spirit, the liberator whose coming his people had always foretold, the Manitouiriniou, the Wonderful Man.

Now the Manitouiriniou said to him, "We are the inhabitants of an ancient house. The forest is our soul. We must always stay together there. But now they cut down the

three-hundred-year-old white pines and our home is reduced to a charnel house."

Peter Coyote still dressed in his ceremonial owl-feather
cloak each year at the summer solstice and assembled with
his brothers and sisters in the lakeside clearing, like a room in
the forest, the great walls of trees rising high on every side.
They performed the Ghost Dance ceremonies which kept
the flame of their spirit alive. Peter Coyote saw no contradic-
tion between these "pagan" ceremonies and his Christian
conversion. He kept up the old ways out of a sense of conti-
nuity and wholeness, an artistic rather than religious duty to
his band. To this end, he invited Billy Sunday to bear witness
as his brother in Christ, as well as his brother in the woods.

Peter Coyote took the young children, even those still in
papooses, into that great room in the forest near the lake.
From far away they heard the thunder of Manitou Falls.
They visited their burial mounds of smooth egglike stones
inscribed with weeping eyes. They took their charcoal and
fire stones, and when the first puff of spirit smoke rose from
the Manitou pipe, there was a cry of jubilation, as the feeling when a spirit is in its own home.

The ceremony began late in the afternoon at that conse-
crated place. Each of them wore a "ghost shirt" of white
cloth. Peter Coyote, as leader, carried the ghost stick, six
feet long, with red cloth and the feathers of a crow, the sacred bird of the Ghost Dance. The dancers were ceremoni-
ally painted, their faces daubed white with clay. They went
into trances and communed with the souls of dead friends.
Afterward, they all went to bathe in the lake, to wash away
all evil acts, past and present.

But that afternoon Peter Coyote saw not his great-grandfather spirit, nor the Manitouiriniou, but a figure he remembered from many years before as Jane Whitecloud. He walked straight up to her, still holding his pipe, and blew smoke on her as an act of homage. He saw the smoke drift through the skin on her chest. He saw the grey foamy substance which leaked from her open mouth. She spoke from her mouth in bolts of lightning, and after she had spoken, her words rumbled away through the forest and joined the thunder of the waterfall. Her mouth twisted, the muscles of her face contorted, and her body arched back. She sank back into forgetfulness and disappeared.

Billy Sunday had spent too long studying his Bible at night, and he had taken lately to wearing wire-rimmed spectacles. When he was absorbed in his reading, the halo of lamplight around his head gave an impression of gentleness, acceptance. Since he had attended the Ghost Dance last summer, the pain in his face, which had begun in the Bower of Beauty even before he was born, had miraculously healed. The lines of anguish around his eyes had been soothed away and the tightness in his mouth unclenched. Billy Sunday's face grew fuller. He looked more like everyone else. As time went by, his face took on the ruddy complexion of one who has survived a shipwreck and dined out too often on the story. This was the look he kept through the period of his ministry, until his death in 1935.

13

FREDERICK JACKSON TURNER

"So," Mae said. "I thought we might begin with clear soup and egg balls. Flounder with sauce tartare. Cucumber and tomato in French dressing. Beef and mushroom sauce. Spinach and potatoes. Ice cream and chocolate cake and coffee after."

"Splendid," said Turner.

How does a man continue to live with a wife who has not the faintest idea who he is? A week after his homecoming to Madison at the end of summer, Mae was arranging a dinner party for the Saturday night. But Fred had proved less than enthusiastic to resume his social obligations. This came to a head on the Thursday evening. They sat at the big oak table in silence, waiting for the maid to carry out the tray with the remains of the meat on it. He felt tenderness for his wife. And God knew she did not mean to irritate him. It was just that she seemed to value above all else her social position, the membership of the Madison Literary Club and the Audubon Society, the invitations to dine at the home of the President of the university, the having of two maids, the spending of $67.30 last month on hats. How could he enter God's mind, when his days and nights were filled with such things? How could the poet of the frontier be born?

Mae was perplexed by the change in her husband when he returned from his summer fishing trip. Instead of coming home healthy and invigorated by life in the great outdoors, he seemed nervous, apprehensive, exhausted. Now she said in a soothing voice, "I know there is something wrong."

Intuition was one of the attributes of womanhood which Turner had always found puzzling. He had built his historian's view of the world from logic. Hypotheses always had to be tested against the evidence. "There is nothing wrong." His voice was controlled, carefully neutral. "I have just got back to work on my paper on the frontier. And I cannot fail but see a dinner party as a darned distraction."

She said gently, "Fred? I want to know all about it."

"About what?"

"The girls, of course. The girls who disappeared."

It had been in all the newspapers. The Balsam Point "disappearances" had been the topic of much discussion among the members of the Madison Literary Club. The favored reading during the past year or so had been the ingenious detective stories by A. Conan Doyle which had recently appeared in *Blackwood's* magazine. In fact,

Turner's idyllic little fishing spot had gained some notoriety from these cases. The disappearances were so mystifying, they had been blamed on supernatural forces and Indian witchcraft.

Now as Turner sat at the table, Mae went upstairs and got the reports she had clipped from the *Wisconsin State Journal*:

> The body of a girl was found in an ice shed behind the inn at Balsam Point in the north of the state. It is believed to be the body of Emma Tenn, from Menominee.

And:

> A reward of one hundred dollars has been offered by the family of Twyla Flake, who disappeared last July near Balsam Point in the north of the state.

And:

> An arrest warrant has been issued for Dr. Anfin the Clairvoyant, also known as the New Necromancer, late of Ringling Bros. Circus. It has been stated by the authorities that Dr. Anfin is no longer associated with the circus. It is believed that Dr. Anfin's trick was to conceal in the cuff of his shirt a pad containing chloral hydrate, and that these "knock-out drops" put his female victims into a trance, during which he would violate them. It is thought that Dr. Anfin has escaped to Canada.

"Dear little Mae. How ghoulish you are. There is nothing to tell. Nothing at all. I saw some of the men searching in the woods one day. But that's all."

"Were they looking for Twyla Flake or Emma Tenn?"

"How on earth would I know? Really, Mae, you seem to be better informed on this subject than I am."

Turner looked down at the pattern of the rug. "A man goes fishing to get away from troubles, not to seek them out."

"Just tell me."

"I said I have nothing to tell."

"Perhaps you prefer to discuss it with someone else. Like your Miss Everest."

"She's not 'my' anything, except my student. And soon to be Doctor Kate Everest, by the way. For God's sake, Kate Everest has nothing whatsoever to do with this."

"Fred, I want you to trust me, confide in me. Like when you told me about when you were a boy and you used to go with that Indian girl in the woods. What was her name? I don't know why I can never remember her name."

Turner left the table as soon as the meal was finished, went into his study and closed the door. His books, journals and maps lay open before him. Safely alone, he unlocked his desk drawer and took out his manuscript to resume work.

He had been invited to submit a paper to a meeting of the American Historical Association which was to take place at the World's Columbian Exposition in Chicago the following July. He had accepted and replied that he would be happy to give a paper on "The Significance of the

Frontier in American History." But there was something hindering progress on his paper, a problem he did not understand.

He got through his days, the usual rounds of the busy young professor at Madison. In the daytime he was alert, vigilant, analytical, but at night it was a different story. He sat up until three in the morning with *Scribner's Statistical Atlas of the United States* open before him. The snow which hid the earth should have brought peace to Turner that winter. He tried to concentrate on his frontier paper, to achieve an orderly arrangement of his ideas, but the Spirit World of Balsam Point continued to beckon to him.

For a couple of hours that night he deceived himself that he was making progress with his paper. The boy who had wanted to be the "poet of the frontier" was still struggling to find voice. Turner's idea of America was a simple one: "The history of America is the development of democracy in connection with free land." He suggested that those geographical features which were unique to the settlement of the United States might have had subtle effects in shaping the national character and institutions.

The maps in his *Scribner's Atlas* told him not only about forests and rivers, but population and income; the richness or barrenness of farming land; which way a particular community had voted in Presidential elections. The topography of America was changing. Rivers were being dammed and new lakes formed; forests were cleared and railroads laid out. There were new maps needed all the time. In the latest Census Report issued in November 1892, the Superintendent of the Census had made a remarkable statement:

> Up to and including 1890 the country had a frontier of settlement, but at present the unsettled area is so broken into by isolated bodies of settlement that there can hardly be said to be a frontier line.

Turner crumpled the latest of his pages and threw it across the room to where it settled with its brothers on the hearth rug in front of the fire. He was miserably aware of his failure to marry the angels of feeling to the boiled cabbage of his ideas.

His ambitions were of the highest order, and even if he were not equal to the task he had set himself, he had to try at least for the sake of his own self-respect. His failure was not due to a lack of willpower. The task could not be achieved solely by dint of exertion or the application of the rational mind. As he sat poring over the population density maps in *Scribner's Atlas*, he heard the squaws in the village on the bank talking in their low excited voices. He heard the beating sticks as they winnowed wild rice directly into the floors of their canoes. He heard the paddle of Jane's canoe beating the water. The frontier he wanted to give expression to could only be understood like music—a unity of place and mind, forest and soul, the lines of an indigo tattoo on tobacco-colored skin—in short, a poetic order of existence. But he knew he must deal only with historical facts.

The lines of settlement, drawn by the steady hand of the anonymous cartographer, began to move and blur in Turner's mind. The pioneering settlements were like the floating islands he had seen in the lake at Balsam Point, great mats of sedge that had broken away from the shore and laid the foundation for trees, solid mats of vegetation whose roots intertwined. They moved to different places around the lake, blown by the wind.

There would be many such nights, in the months to come, when Turner sat up late, smoking in his den, listening to the murmurs of the girls in the forest. A rotting corpse and a beautiful voice. A poem of madness and death. These were the conditions under which his idea of America was made. How was the historian to redeem the facts of settlement from this nightmare? How was it that the woods were *already* full of such disturbing dreams?

He took up his pen, dipped it in ink and swept across the smooth paper. The nib made a scratching sound which was particularly satisfying. He could feel the slight resistance of the grain of the paper through the barrel of the pen. It felt as though another hand were guiding his.

He wrote of "the edge of free land" and "the graphic line which records the expansive energies of the people behind it . . ." American social development was continually beginning anew on the frontier. The influence of the native Indians retarded civilization, "compelling society to organize and consolidate in order to hold the frontier." It was just two years since the massacre at Wounded Knee had taken place. The frontier constituted "the meeting ground between savagery and civilization." All that is significant in American life was born on the extreme edge of things:

> From the conditions of frontier life came intellectual traits of profound importance . . . That coarse-

ness and strength combined with acuteness and inquisitiveness; the practical, inventive turn of mind, quick to find expedients; that masterful grasp of material things, lacking in the artistic but powerful to effect great ends; that restless, nervous energy; that dominant individualism . . . Since the days when the fleet of Columbus sailed into the waters of the New World, America has been another name for opportunity, and the people of the United States have taken their tone from the incessant expansion which has not only been open but has even been forced upon them . . . For a moment, at the frontier, the bonds of custom are broken and unrestraint is triumphant.

Turner leaned back in his chair and closed his eyes. The ancient cedars appeared again before him, reflected on the surface of the lake, and their spicy smell filled the air. Turner crossed the dream line and was back in the trees again. *Unrestraint is triumphant* . . . His blood chilled when he recalled the glimpse of the figure in Temple Woods, its long matted hair, its ball of a forehead, its morning suit in rags. And another time in the forest, when Billy Sunday had been watching Pauline sing, the way he had been moving, as if he was being ridden by devils, and not just harmlessly masturbating behind a tree.

By an extension of character, Billy Sunday now expanded in Turner's imagination from an ideal frontier type met at Balsam Point during a summer's fishing to a kind of solution, a symbol. Turner recalled the look in Billy Sunday's eyes as he had stood outside the window and watched

Pauline sing. What had he seen in the room to move his heart in such a sublime way? Billy Sunday had seemed to float in the lamplight, as though he were bathed in the light of God. It was like he had glimpsed the beginning of a fresh new world.

Turner had wanted to create a world of wonder, a poem which revealed the hidden forces shaping American life and institutions, a secret order of existence, hitherto unsuspected, born in the woods of the Pilgrims, and which continued to grow and change through all the frontier stages. He struggled to keep believing that he could still hear the old hymn, Walt Whitman's "greatest poem." That look of absolute faith in Billy Sunday's eyes seemed like a sign.

Turner now knew that his idea of America could be redeemed only through those eyes, with their look of hope and longing. This boy who thought of the woods as a soul had a singular kind of innocence before God. In those first woods, Thoreau's and Emerson's idea of America had come to its pinnacle.

But Turner knew there was another America, a stain on the soul of the frontier experience which drove men mad with shame. Hitherto, Turner had emphasized only the positive effects of the frontier. Now the dark dream of America he had denied had begun to seep into his history, quite independent of his own intentions, different from anything he wanted his "poem of America" to be. The nightmare existed beyond his own making, pushing up through the floor of the forest.

Now Turner felt himself sinking back into the darkness. He hardly knew anything that was going on around him. He was back on the forest floor again the day he had been fishing and looked up to see the boy running along the ancestral trail, striped by bars of sunlight. Billy Sunday's eyes were full of terror and light. Turner wondered now if the boy's terror had been caused just by the discovery of that unclean place, the Indian burial ground among the hemlocks; or whether, coming upon the tortured shapes of one tree's roots in particular, Billy Sunday had seen the shade of his mother rising from the earth.

Near midnight, Turner put on his coat and strolled through the frozen streets of Madison. He passed a house with a lamp in the window: some student cramming desperately for an examination; perhaps even one of his own students. He felt nostalgic for that urgency, passion, conviction. And the unseen student working in the night made him feel guilty about his own unfinished paper. As he stood and smoked at the edge of frozen Lake Mendota, at the boatshed at the bottom of Frances Street, he heard the murmuring of the wind over the ice from the State Hospital on the far shore. He felt a manic impulse, an urge to perform some simple irrevocable act which might change his life course completely. But he could not yet understand what was required of him.

Turner tried to break the spell, but all the time now his thoughts returned to the forest, to the attic room at Balsam Point, and to the gloomy interior of the ice shed, the "room without windows." He was back in Temple Woods again. The late afternoon sun threw the shadows of trees across the trail in sudden violent pulses. From the unseen lake came the chugging of the wood-burning steamer, *The Lady of the Lake*. He heard Pauline singing through the trees. The notes fell away in a great sigh, a sound full of such yearning it had brought tears to Billy Sunday's eyes. The injustice of Billy Sunday, his son, being dead in the lake, had got under his skin, and lived on with every beat of his pulse, deep in his blood, something that made him aboriginal, older than the pilgrims.

The worst of it was finally to lie beside his sleeping wife, sleepless, unable to stop trembling. He could feel the warm weight of her rump nestled close against his stomach. Even in her sleep the poor thing was trying to comfort him, whereas he would have preferred that she hated him outright. He flirted with the idea of a confession, a release from this intolerable burden of guilt. But what could he confess? A denial of love? His paternity of a boy now dead? Was there anything he could say that she would understand as not his admission of personal guilt but of the broken faith of his countrymen? She would laugh at him. He wanted to see her pretty little face screwed up in rage and hatred. He wanted to feel her little fists thumping into his chest.

It it not through fear of the nightmare, but fear he will enjoy it, fear he will transgress in his dreams, that he shakes his head in a vain effort to keep himself awake. Turner's spiky wakefulness imitates the Pilgrim Fathers, who constructed around their little settlements a defense of pickets to keep the bewitching wilderness at bay. The sight of a girls' naked back kept reappearing to him, and he kept shaking himself awake, fearing that he might in sleep turn in the bed and whisper a name.

Another hour passed and he could still feel the heavy warmth of Mae's sleeping body in the bed beside him. With his head resting against the cedar headboard, he smoked a cigarette, watching the magical wreaths of smoke drift above him in the near dark. At last Turner wandered in the night beyond his own little picket fence, to he knew not where, as the dreamer steps from a cliff's edge into the chasm, into darkness. He wandered among the black shining trees, and experienced again the feeling of furtive excitement, the sense of possibility, the promise of lulling movement. Among the passing faces was one face he always had to pursue with his questions. In these dreams he saw again the milk maid, Emma Tenn, staring at him in her brazen way, as she had so many times in the evenings, when he had taken his catch to store in the ice shed. The blonde hair was drawn back from her pale, delicate face. Then, as if in a photographic negative, her face and her hair grew darker, her expression changed. She became the face of another. The muscles of her face began to twitch, her mouth twisted and she seemed to have difficulty breathing. Then her features began to dissolve, like old emulsion on a glass plate, and the face melted back into the darkness. Turner slept.

He was awakened by a sudden harsh sound and an explosion of light. Mae, already dressed, had opened the bedroom drapes. He stared up at her, sweating, helpless.

In the December of 1892, Woodrow Wilson paid Turner a visit. They had been friends since Turner's days of graduate school at Johns Hopkins, where Wilson had been a visiting professor in the spring term. After dinner, the two men sat in Turner's den with their whiskey, and from habit they began to argue good-naturedly about history and politics. Turner outlined his "frontier theory" to his friend.

"I have come to see that statement of the Superintendent of the Census as being of the utmost importance—'there can hardly be said to be a frontier line.' Until now it has been the availability of free land at the edge of civilization, its continuous recession, western movement, which explain American development. But now look around you at the countryside. Farmers in poverty, people going mad and shooting their families and themselves, all this burning of barns. Something has changed in our national life. It is the end of our old idea of America."

"You are an idealist, Fred. You talk about the importance of free land at the border of civilization. But I think there is a kind of romantic yearning about your wilderness. Did these insights into the greatness and dignity of our nation occur to you at that little fishing spot of yours? What's it called—Balsam Point?"

Turner smiled and said he had spent every day of the summer flicking a carefully tied fly over one or another of the dreamy pools to be found there. He confessed, "I am ashamed of myself at the end of every summer, when I think how very little I have worked. It is a bad habit I have gotten into."

"And did the good wife mind you being away all that time? She has little Jackson Allen and Dorothy to care for, you know."

"Mae doesn't mind my fishing. Not in the least. Why should she? Every man has a need to break away from the women for a spell. There's something about the great outdoors that agrees with a man. A spell from petticoat government." Then Turner burst out, "Women are so—unrealistic! Our wives don't want to know about the world. They want everything sanitized and bowdlerized and made fit for consumption by the Ladies Guild! Don't try to explain anything to them!"

"Whatever are you talking about?"

"I can't help feeling that there is a true point of view in the history of this nation which we have not yet discovered. We feel it—oh yes—like poetry, or music. Do you know what I mean? What no other man can know about you. What you hardly dare to know about yourself. Because we will not allow ourselves to know it."

"Well, Fred. Your fishing spot must be an idyllic place from which to contemplate western movement and the greatness of our democratic institutions."

"You think I lack sound historical method?"

"I think you are very courageous."

"A man with more intellect might possess less courage?"

"On the contrary. You are brave and intellectual both."

"Well, I suppose it is something at least to want to have a great idea."

"That's true," said his friend. "And I think that you will have your great idea, and that you will become a most re-markable man because of it."

Suddenly Turner heard himself saying, "When I first went to Balsam Point all those years ago, I was still an ideal-ist. But not now. No. Not now."

Wilson looked at him for a long time with a puzzled, concerned look on his face; then shook his head and let out an indulgent laugh, as if resigning himself to a matter utterly beyond redress. "Yes. I think you are a very remarkable man."

By the early summer of 1893, Turner was still struggling to finish his paper. Each day on his way from the library to class he passed the inscription on a plaque on Bascom Hill: WHATEVER MAY BE THE LIMITATIONS WHICH TRAMMEL INQUIRY ELSEWHERE, WE BELIEVE THAT THE GREAT STATE UNIVERSITY OF WISCONSIN SHOULD EVER ENCOURAGE THAT CONTINUAL AND FEARLESS SIFTING AND WINNOWING BY WHICH ALONE THE TRUTH CAN BE FOUND. But for Turner it was not as easy as that.

He walked past the medical laboratories at the university. In a hall of the Faculty of Medicine, experimental inoculations were being conducted by Board of Health officials. An odor of methylated spirit came from the corridors. It reminded him of Robertson's smell. Turner had read by chance about the business of mortuaries selling bodies for medical research. The most famous case was that of Burke in 1827; but there had been more recent cases of "Burkism" in Chicago. He wondered about those girls who had disappeared, whose bodies had never been found. Lately, without really knowing why, Turner had found himself quite often walking past the Anatomy lecture rooms with their faint smell of vivisection.

He was tired, and by three o'clock he was at the boathouse at the bottom of Frances Street. He carried his

Old Town canoe down to the shore and entered the sparkling net of sunshine on Lake Mendota.

When he was paddling on the other side of the lake, near Governor's Island and the asylum, he was surprised to hear the chug-chug of a wood-burning steamer pass close by, the splashing of the paddlewheel, like an arm repeatedly beating the water. When he looked around him, the surface of the lake reflected blank, unbroken sky. A shroud of smoke covered the shore, as if to discourage intruders. He laid down his paddle and drifted for a while with his eyes closed and it was then that he heard the voice of Pauline L'Allemand again. He recognized the aria from *Don Giovanni.* It was the same pure, soaring voice he had heard so many times the previous year at Balsam Point and he knew that in hearing her voice, he was once again hearing the voice of his own destiny.

Earlier that week he had received a letter from Robert Robertson, Assistant Superintendent of Pinkerton's Detective Agency in Chicago:

Dear Friend Turner, You will of course recall the "disappearances" of girls which have taken place at Balsam Point the past few years. I believe you were even involved in, shall we call it, some extraordinary communications upon the subject. You will also remember the case of Emma Tenn, the girl in the ice shed. I have received some news on the subject which I am sure will be of interest to you . . .

Turner landed his canoe and walked along the cinder path toward the redbrick buildings of the asylum. Nurses propelled human shapes in wooden bathing chairs along the paths in the rose garden. Turner looked at those forms of human misery, the hunched dark souls who might have been dreamed by Temple Woods, with their twisted faces, fearful, rocking repetitively back and forth as if to soothe or lull the pain of the economic crisis and the failure that had led them to this place. These phantoms had all been shaped by history.

As Turner walked toward the big redbrick building with its barred upper windows, he heard a sound like a parrot shrieking from the wards inside. Some distance away he could hear music being played. He crossed the sunlit lawn and saw Edgar with his aluminum violin, playing with a group of other inmates who had formed themselves into a band. He still wore his blue silk waistcoat, and as he cradled the violin into his neck he had a gallant smile on his face.

The Director informed Turner that the L'Allemands had been admitted to Mendota the previous winter, both mother and son suffering from "delusions and mania." He looked up their entries in the Blue Book in which the details of all admissions were recorded. They were so poor they only had their stage clothes left. They had formed the conviction that their neighbors at Balsam Point were persecuting them, coming into their house and shooting at the keys on the piano. Moreover, Pauline had begun making the most wild and defamatory statements against all manner of individuals concerning the disappearances of the girls at Balsam Point. She had publicly accused two brothers, Moses and Jacob Rhinelander, and it had ended in a wild scene. No one believed a word she said anymore. Such baseless and irresponsible accusations were brought to the attention of the law. Pauline and Edgar had been committed to Mendota as much for their own protection as anything else. At least here they could be properly fed and looked after.

Pauline L'Allemand was kept in a locked room. Soon after she arrived here, she had taken an insane dislike to one of the other patients, Poitr Romanovich, and had attacked him with a pair of sewing scissors. Since then, she had been locked away for the safety of the others.

Sometimes there was a sudden explosion of voice from Pauline's cell, a singing of such passion and violence as to startle anyone who happened to be walking along the corridor at that time. No one except Edgar visited her in there. He delivered the food tray and emptied the latrine bucket, and she preferred to live in her own world as much as any monk or hermit. Edgar, on the other hand, seemed to get on quite well with the other patients. Edgar, with his limp and his good-natured smile, played violin with the band.

One more thing, the Director said. Turner was not the first visitor to request an interview with Pauline. Just the previous week, a man called Robertson, of the Pinkerton's office in Chicago, had come here to talk with her.

Pauline's room was furnished in the most severe fashion. The walls had been painted the dull color of burlap. The shades were drawn, so that Turner did not at first see the form of the person standing against the wall. She had more the look of a prisoner than a patient. Then she pulled open the shades and the sun filled her room with light. She wore the gown, now old and torn, in which she had once appeared on the opera stages of Europe. The upper half had been sewn with sequins and the sunlight made it dazzling, theatrical, as if she had attracted more than her fair share of sunlight.

Turner could tell immediately that she had fallen into the habits of madness. She stared at him openly, rudely. She examined his face skeptically, as though she might have recognized him from a long time in the past. Her mouth hung open, her eyes watery, and she breathed harshly. Then she lifted the back of her hand and wiped away the tears and all at once she seemed to come to her senses. "I must look after Edgar," she said. "My poor Edgar. He has not been very well. I was always terrified that he might find his father. When we arrived here and he saw the old man, Edgar seemed to know right away it was him. There was a bond between them. It was as though Edgar knew instinctively the Old Necromancer would use his powers to protect him in this evil place. I watched them together, from this window, teasing the other patients, inventing new acts of petty cruelty. But Edgar was always like that, especially where girls were concerned. It seems his nature knows no other than the cruelest way."

Turner stood at the window in her room looking back

over Lake Mendota toward the university on the other shore, turning over in his mind those scenes from another time. The dark world of the trees continued to speak through Pauline in that grim room with its carbolic smell. Her face had aged under the veil of the forest. Deep lines like scars ran down her cheeks. Her eyes flashed as she explained why she had falsely accused Billy Sunday. Her cracked lips opened and the words finally came out.

In the morning the lake had been still shrouded with fog. The sun rose, red and terrifying, from the lake. Edgar stood at the ice shed behind the inn, chin tilted up above his soft white collar, cigar clenched between his teeth, fingers fumbling at the buttons of his fly, a look of benign expectation on his face. There was someone standing in the shadows inside the ice shed watching him. This was the place where he had seen Jenny Four-Fingers slip the bolt and disappear inside, to steal fish. But it was not Jenny Four-Fingers who had gone into the ice shed. It was a white girl, yellow-haired, scarcely fifteen years old. It was the Swiss girl, Emma Tenn, who had finished the early morning milking and had taken the milk pails to the ice shed.

Then he noticed there was a patch of melted yellow ice on the floor of the ice shed, which was still steaming. Edgar thought about that. There were piles of sawdust and maple chips stored inside the big heavy door and a snow shovel resting against the wall. The smell of fish was strong in the ice shed; it was where sportsmen stored their catch. Edgar stood there, wondering about that yellow hole in the ice. It was then he heard a voice talking to him strangely. The voice had been in his head since he had awakened, but until then he had managed to ignore it. But now it would not be ignored. The voice in his head was telling him the milk maid was so lazy she had just taken a piss in there and that he ought to kill the girl for it.

14

FREDERICK JACKSON TURNER

It was July again, the time of year when it was Turner's habit to pack his fly-rod and rucksack and head north to Balsam Point. But this year he would not be going to sit by the lakeside in his usual way.

The Congress of Historians at the World's Columbian Exposition in Chicago opened on July 10, 1893. Turner and Mae had traveled by train from Madison with a group of friends and colleagues, the Reuben Gold Thwaiteses, the C. L. Hendricksons, and the Charles Homer Haskinses. They took rooms in a dormitory of the University of Chicago near the fair site and Turner attended the opening sessions of the Committee on Historical Literature in Room 24 of the new Art Institute. But even by that late stage Turner still had not finished writing his paper.

While the others were visiting the attractions of the World's Fair, he locked himself away in a final struggle to get the words out.

Wednesday July 12 was hot. An invitation had been extended to historians attending the conference to visit Buffalo Bill's Wild West Show that afternoon. Turner knew he should have stayed in the dormitory, making some last-minute revisions to his paper, but could not resist the chance to listen to the famous man. Turner and his friends walked by the lake's edge, where there was a cool afternoon breeze, and watched the arrival of the replica of a Viking ship from Norway.

There were many "Buffalo Bills" in those years, turning up in small towns, giving lectures and performances. Colonel William Cody now printed "Buffalo Bill Himself" on his advertising posters.

Buffalo Bill was dressed in buckskin with fringed sleeves, and held his famous rifle in his hands, the 50-caliber breech-loading Springfield he had used to fell more than four thousand buffaloes. He chopped and changed his subject. He began to talk about General Custer and the Little Big Horn, then about his duel with Chief Yellow Hand. "Boy," he said. "I brought Yellow Hand down with my rifle, a clean shot, right in the middle of the belly. So there he is, waiting for me on the ground like that, the stomach wound spreading dark across the buckskin, waiting for me to come and finish him off, but still with the knife in his hand. But I already had my hunting knife out. Within seconds I had driven that keen-edged weapon to its hilt in his heart. Jerking his war bonnet off, I scientifically scalped him in about five seconds."

That night when Turner mounted the podium to present his paper on "The Significance of the Frontier in American History," the audience had already listened to four scholarly papers. His friend Dr. Reuben Gold Thwaites had spoken on "Early Lead Mining in Illinois and Wisconsin." Turner's paper was greeted with polite applause, but Turner knew his audience had already been bored to death.

Though it might not have felt like it at the time, that night in Chicago was the beginning of a new phase in his life. Fame did not come suddenly to Turner, but steadily. The following year, 1894, he and Mae bought land at 629 Frances Street, nearly on the shore of Lake Mendota, and had a fine two-story house built. He was given expanded responsibilities in the History Department, and on April 27, 1894, their third child, a daughter, was born. Turner might have been forgiven for believing he had finally defeated the darkness of Temple Woods.

The one cause of conflict between the Turners was religion. Turner consistently refused to accompany his wife to church. One day in 1896 Mae requested that her husband accompany her to a Revival meeting. Turner's mouth showed irritation. He said, "Oh me, oh my," and quickly found an excuse. Mae often got religious like this. She liked her religion to be sticky with sentiment. "I guess I'll be going by myself, then," she said. The prayer meeting was to take place in the football stadium, by candlelight, on the Friday evening. It was to be addressed by a young evangelist who was causing quite a stir. More than three hundred people were expected to attend.

It was only when he learned the name of the young preacher, and saw his likeness on the lithograph posters around Madison, that Turner understood what had really happened back there in the lake, and realized that he too, as well as Billy Sunday, had been afforded a kind of reprieve.

Even so, he did not accompany Mae to the Revival meeting. There are some feelings in life so terrible we do not even dare try to confront them. Turner decided to keep his secret, protect it, seal it up dark in his heart.

Six years passed.

During those years, with his fine new house, a happy domestic life, a contented wife and three children, it might have seemed to Turner that the world was in its first morning, and the pathways of his life were again full of light.

But Turner would still wake in the night and know that in his sleep he had been back there in the forest, with the branches shivering overhead. The smell of her was in the bedroom, and he knew that secretly, in the night, something was infecting the good order of his life, like the stains he had seen on the glass photographic plates, like the spreading of the diphtheria epidemics.

In the north of the state, a mill closed, rivers and streams were fished out and a tiny timber village became a ghost town. Soon there would be no one left to remember Balsam Point as it had been in 1892 when a photographer and an opera singer had gone to a house in the forest to draw the shades and entertain phantoms and try to shut the real world out. There would be no one to remember how many mornings a man at the old inn rose at dawn and took his fly-rod with him to the river, walking through the wet grass, with the mosquitoes rising in the pearling light. There would be no one left to remember those girls who disappeared. From time to time, hunters or a gang of loggers would find another body in the woods, the damp springtime revealing what had been buried under the snow, the old shapes pushing up from the dark world. Not Twyla Flake, though. Her body had never been found.

The historian's true enemy is time itself. Time, with its heartless relativism, its violent apathy, quells the sense of mortal outrage. Events rot away like corpses, their traces ever fainter in the earth, the fingerprints of the sinner ever more difficult to detect. Until all that's left are the faint stains of outrage which surround the sites of crimes.

Time.

Had Edgar L'Allemand killed Twyla Flake as well as the milk maid? Or, Turner wondered, could it have been Edgar's father, Romanovich, the Old Necromancer, or even his successor, Dr. Anfin, one of the various, ever-possible incarnations of the Necromancer, the stain on the soul, the snake in the garden?

And, Turner sometimes also wondered, what of that taciturn, secretive photographer who had disappeared from the scene just at the crucial moment? Apparently, Van Schaick was still living a quiet family life in Black River Falls, still taking his conventional studio portraits at twenty-five cents a shot.

Van Schaick had often been alone in Temple Woods that summer and knew the trails well. For that matter, what of

Turner himself? What of his own secret, the smell of decay in the forest, his own interior world so dark and savage he could not even now let it push up into conscious thought?

Soon Turner too would be gone and what would be left to remember him by? A few books to be attacked by the young and ambitious, like moths. He would have disappeared entirely into the sands of time. No one would know his secrets. How would they be able to discover them? Just one more secret buried among the untold millions. If Turner had learned anything at all as an historian, it is this: We can never tell what anyone's true motives are, not even our own. We can dig and dig into the well of intention, but the bucket keeps coming up with a brown-colored trickle of lies in the bottom.

Historians have a tendency to overdetermine the past. From a distance in time, when the people are dead, their lives seem fixed, settled, unchanging. It's all too easy to forget the strangeness of things. We cannot know precisely where our own deepest interest resides. We cannot be sure whether it lies in the "facts" of the events, or somewhere in our own lost interior worlds, inarticulate, yet still alive. We are looking through the wrong end of the telescope. *"What no man can know about you. What you hardly dare to know about yourself."*

Gradually the world had lost interest in who had been the dark spouse of Twyla Flake among the vast silent trees stretching into Canada. It is dangerous to inquire too much into these things. They spread like a stain in the vaults of our own deepest silences, our most private exaltations.

Then, in 1899, just as the century was drawing to a close, its secrets safely buried, catastrophe struck in Turner's life.

That winter was colder than usual in Madison. Temperatures of thirty below zero were recorded. In February there was another outbreak of diphtheria. Such was the severity of the epidemic, the schools in Madison were closed and a quarantine of infected households was enforced. Turner's youngest child, six-year-old Mae Sherwood, caught diphtheria early in the month and, on February 11, she died.

Turner and Mae tried to cope with their grief. The snows of that terrible February melted, summer came again, but Turner did not flee civilization and journey back to the forests and streams of northern Wisconsin that year.

Then in the fall, in October, the seven-year-old Jackson Allen Turner developed severe abdominal pain. His appendix ruptured and inflammation set in. A doctor from Chicago was sent for, but it was too late. On October 22, a Sunday afternoon, Turner's son died. There was only nine-year-old Dorothy left.

Mae, his wife, suffered a complete nervous collapse. She could not accept what had happened and she simply went out of her mind. She was taken away to a sanatorium in Chicago. Not until the June of 1900 would she be well enough to return home.

Turner's grief crushed him. "I have not done anything, and have not the heart to do anything," he wrote to a friend. He walked the streets of Madison late at night, a lonely figure making his way up State Street, turning left onto Frances to the home where there was no happiness or warmth now. When he spoke at all, his mouth filled with the bitter injustice of what had happened and choked him.

The first epoch of his life had closed. He would never be the same man again. His face showed the burden of time and pain, the way America had suddenly come to seem like a different place. There was less blueness in Turner's eyes, as if their light had leaked away somewhere. He had just turned thirty-eight, but he already looked old, like those times he was rowing on Lake Mendota and the wind shriveled up his face. His pain darkened the landscape of his life like a stain leaking into the new century.

A man was sitting on an orange crate on Lake Mendota at the very end of the nineteenth century. He might have been just another fisherman sitting there in his dungarees and lumberjacket. It was a winter's afternoon, the last day of December, and the skin was drawn tight on his face. It followed the carved ridges of bone, making his head seem skull-like. Turner was often to be found here, having walked out from his home at the end of Frances Street, staring across the ice toward the dark line of trees on the far shore, as though waiting for someone.

The usual crowd had walked out from Madison, wearing their plaid lumberjackets and woolen caps. They spent the freezing hours sitting on upturned sleds, on crates and boxes. Some carried stoves and even tents onto the ice. They sed a heavy ice pick to make a hole in the ice, eighteen inches thick, and set their seventy-foot lines baited with salmon eggs and perch eyes. Some nights there were three thousand of these bundled figures out on Lake Mendota, crouched over their fishing holes, circles of faces lit by their lanterns.

A couple of students sitting outside the nearest fraternity house began to talk, their voices scarcely audible. One of them suddenly straightened and let out a muffled exclamation. He must have got a fright when the figure loomed up at them out of the dusk. The ghost passed them without speaking. "Who's that?" the student asked.

"That's Turner. He comes here every day and just sits. Hasn't taught his classes all year."

"Something happened to him, I guess."

"Something happened, right. Two little children dead in a year. Now there's only one left. His poor wife is off in the sanatorium in Chicago. They say she hears the little ones' voices. They say she hears their speech in the woods."

It was still several hours before the people of Madison would gather in State Street and grasp strangers' hands and howl like wolves in the ghostly light of a First of January moon. It was, after all, the one night of the century when university professors and bank presidents could for a few hours forget to be respectable citizens and let their hair down. And so the students sat and drank from bottles outside their fraternity houses at the edge of Lake Mendota. Out on the frozen lake lanterns had been lighted, and the darkness there was tucked with points of light, seeds of light, like stars. From somewhere came the thumping of a steam engine, and the sounds of animals in the fairgrounds;

or perhaps it was the unquiet murmuring of the inmates of the asylum, three miles across the ice from the university.

Later that night, Turner walked back down Frances Street to the frozen lake. When he was about a mile across, he looked back at the lights of Madison, the great forest in the snow ahead, the dark trees like fur upon the white land, the snowy forgetful expanses. He saw the circles of faces of the fishermen around the lanterns. But there was something else. Something out there in the blue night was moving.

He saw the ancient cedars rise again in the mirror of the lake, their spicy smell filling the air. At the lake shore, in the misty trees, there was a figure, a ghostly observer of everything that had passed within Van Schaick's chronicles of glass. Then he heard, faintly, as if from a long time ago, another sound. It was not the pure voice of Pauline singing. It was a raw voice, corded with suffering, the sound of something still untamed, savage, original: avenging wolves born in Jane Whitecloud's rioting heart. Turner listened to the howls across the lake, as if they were the last organ chord of the hymn of the frontier expiring.

The howls were speaking not from the asylum but from the tundra beyond the trees, from history, a landscape as dark as the night. For a moment more he could hear the thumping of the steam engine, the distressed sounds of the circus animals; then everything went quiet. Until all that was left was a face in a dead photographer's plate, like an imprint upon a shroud, and spectral stains composed of them all; all of us trapped in the glass.

AUTHOR'S NOTE

Most of the people in this novel really existed. More precisely, my characters bear the names of people who once really existed. They are not intended, however, to be portraits of actual historical persons.

My interest in Frederick Jackson Turner dates back twenty years to an undergraduate essay I wrote on the genesis of Turner's "frontier theory." The frontier theory was never quite convincing to me. It seemed not so much a hypothesis as a romantic urge which concealed its own sources and omissions. It is ironic that Turner's paper was published in 1893, a year of rural depression so severe that historians have referred to it as a "psychic crisis" in American life.

My interest was sparked again in 1990 when I was living

on Vancouver Island for a few months. The Canadian writer Mark Jarman loaned me a copy of *Wisconsin Death Trip* by Michael Lesy (New York: Pantheon, 1973; reprinted New York: Anchor Books/Doubleday, 1991), which consists of a collection of Charles Van Schaick's photographs and excerpts from the *Badger State Banner*, Black River Falls, for the years 1885–1900. The haunted quality of the faces in those photographs at the end of the frontier period reminded me that the great tradition in the American novel is a dark, gothic tradition; whereas the myth of the trailblazing frontier is full of light.

Frederick Jackson Turner: Historian, Scholar, Teacher, a biography by Ray Allen Billington (New York: Oxford University Press, 1973), provided me with the bare bones of a life into which I might breathe my imaginary character. The actual Turner, by all accounts a decent fellow, did accompany his father to the pineries in 1877 and 1879. He did suffer a mysterious illness in 1879. He did marry Mae Sherwood Turner, and two of their children, Jackson Allen and Mae Sherwood, did die in 1899. But any resemblance ends with these correspondences of time and place. It is not my intention to defame or vilify the real Turner on a personal level. Rather, I have attempted to unleash an imagined unconscious of his "frontier theory." This is a novel, not a work of history, not a polemic.

There really were a Pauline and Edgar L'Allemand, though they arrived in Black River Falls some twenty years later than the characters in this novel. They did end up in the Mendota asylum, but the details of their lives sketched out in *Wisconsin Death Trip* suggest they were quite different from the characters in this book who bear their names. Charles Van Schaick was of course also an actual person, but for the purposes of my story I have invented him afresh. I have drawn on all these historical sources as imaginative springboards. The novelist, like the high-diver and unlike the historian, takes liberties with the laws of gravity.

There was also an actual Billy (William Ashley) Sunday. He was born in Ames, Iowa, in 1862 (making him sixteen years older than "my" Billy Sunday). His father was killed in the Civil War, he spent four years in an orphanage, and he worked as an undertaker's assistant and a professional baseball player before becoming a famous evangelist in the 1890s. He died in 1935. That is all I know—or wanted to know—about the real Billy Sunday. There was even a Lalla Rookh, advertised as "The Most Beautiful Woman in the World," but her relation to Jane Whitecloud, to Billy Sunday, and to Turner is purely fictitious.

Charles Van Schaick died in 1946, and some thirty thousand of his glass plate negatives were acquired by the Jackson County Historical Society. Even today there are rumors in Black River Falls about a secret collection of "bathing pictures." It has been alleged that in the 1950s an unknown number of these plates were deliberately destroyed by lady members of the Jackson County Historical Society who thought the nudes obscene. In 1958, 2,238 of Van Schaick's glass plates were selected for the State Historical Society of Wisconsin by Paul Vanderbilt, Curator of Iconography. It is there, in the Iconographic Collections of the State Historical Society of Wisconsin in Madison, that the Van Schaick Collection is housed.

The Collection, open to the public, consists of not only the glass plates but also dozens of boxes of photo prints. One writes the box number one wishes to examine on a slip of paper and sits at a table to wait. In due course the box is brought out, along with a pair of white cotton gloves, which must be worn to examine the photographs. I put on the white gloves and carefully examined many boxes of prints. There are portraits, family scenes, chronicles of small-town life, harvests, floods, visiting circuses. On some of the old glass plates the emulsion has degenerated and these flaws show in the prints as shadowy motes and amoebas, mysterious stains.

I went to Black River Falls to look at the Jackson County Historical Society's collection of photographs. Their museum is housed in the old redbrick building where Van Schaick had his studio for sixty years, near the corner of First and Main. Upstairs, I looked through the window where Van Schaick must have stood. A boy who was helping his grandfather, the museum's director, that Saturday morning took me into a back room where there were shelves full of boxes of photo prints. When I showed an interest, he brought down box after box of photographs of Indians for me to see. These were indeed Van Schaick's private snapshots documenting the living conditions among the local Winnebago people, and of all the Van Schaick photos I had looked at, it was these which stayed with me and put down roots into the imagination. Ultimately, in the novel I had Van Schaick taking photos of Ojibwa people, for geographical consistency with my fictional Balsam Point.

As I was driving out of Black River Falls, I passed an old house where a present-day photographer has his studio. The sign at the front of the house announced the name of the business: SPIRIT PHOTOGRAPHY.

ROD JONES

Queenscliff, September 1994